THE GREEN POPINJAYS

ELEANOR FAIRBURN

Strong-willed, beautiful and unwilling to be shackled by the conventions of King or Church, Lady Lucia de Thweng is a law unto herself.

Dubbed the notorious 'Helen of Cleveland', her behaviour scandalised northern England in a time of political change and social upheaval. Against a backdrop of civil war and the tumultuous reins of kings Edward I and II, *The Green Popinjays* tells the true story of a little-known woman in history, bringing Lucia to glorious life, as she fights for her honour and the men she loves.

The Green Popinjays

ELEANOR FAIRBURN

First published in 1962
by Hodder and Stoughton Ltd., London

All rights reserved
© Eleanor Fairburn 1962

This paperback edition first published in 2021
by the Fairburn Estate

This paperback edition produced by KB Conversions, Norwich, United
Kingdom 2021

Cover Illustration & Design copyright Patrick Knowles 2021

The right of Eleanor Fairburn to be identified as author of this work has
been asserted in accordance with Section 77 of the Copyright, Designs
and Patents act 1988

This book is copyright material and must not be copied, reproduced,
transferred, leased, licensed or publicly performed or used in any way
except as specifically permitted in writing by the publishers, as allowed
under the terms and conditions under which it was purchased or as
strictly permitted by applicable copyright law. Any unauthorised
distribution or use of this text may be a direct infringement of the
author's and publisher's rights, and those responsible may be liable in
law accordingly.

ELEANOR Fairburn (1928 – 2015) was born in Westport, Co. Mayo, Ireland. She was educated at St. Louis Convent, Balla and went on to train in Fashion, Art and Design in Dublin. After moving to England, she supplemented her income by writing articles and stories for newspapers, as well as producing knitwear designs for Vogue and Harper's Bazaar.

She settled in North Yorkshire with her husband and daughter, and began her career as a novelist in earnest. Her first book, 'The Green Popinjays' was published in 1962, followed by her most successful book 'The White Seahorse' (1964) about the infamous pirate queen Grace O'Malley.

In all, she wrote 17 works of historical fiction as well as crime thrillers under various pseudonyms, including Emma Gayle, Catherine Carfax, Elena Lyons, and Anna Neville. Alongside her work as a novelist, she taught a writing course sponsored by the University of Leeds, and was also a founding member of the Middlesbrough Writers' Group.

After the death of her husband Brian in 2011, she moved to Norfolk to be closer to her daughter, Anne-Marie. Eleanor Fairburn died peacefully in Norwich on 2nd January, 2015 at the age of 86.

FOREWORD

What marks the infamous life of Lady Lucia de Thweng is its complexity – the sorting of rumour from truth. Her story is an ambitious first novel for a young writer to undertake, but what initially drew Fairburn to it was its setting: Yorkshire. An Irish native, she had moved to Yorkshire to be with her husband, and as an artist and designer was fascinated by the many old castles and their one-time chatelaines. At first drawing on museum pamphlets and historical church records, her research would take her all over Yorkshire, as well as to the dusty archives of the British Library, where Lucia de Thweng lay waiting to be rediscovered.

In her heyday, Lucia was a notorious celebrity. Her escapades, lovers, fashions and faux-pas entertained and alarmed the North of England and the English Court under King Edward I. Fairburn's remarkable sensitivity for bringing across the essence of this woman, rather than the persona, is what makes *The Green Popinjays* such an accomplished book of the genre. It breathes life into a figure long-forgotten, and brings near the emotions, worries and cares of a woman living in a world ruled by church and King – with mortal consequences if your loyalties lay on the wrong side.

Fairburn's love of fashion is apparent in her vivid descriptions of the age's clothing, and the attention to exquisite historical detail. There is a rich texture and sensuous feel to Lucia's life and character that suit her hedonistic life so perfectly. It is odd that, although she was dubbed 'Helen of Cleveland' for her antics, her stories have not been more disseminated in popular culture. In fact, the main works on the life of Lady "Lucy" de Thweng, are the more racy journal articles in Boydell & Brewer, on the laws of Divorce and Adultery in the 14th Century.

Eleanor Fairburn was an author ahead of her time: her works of female-focussed historical fiction were at the forefront of a lasting trend. Her strength was letting the characters shape the story, rather than the historical events. Each of her novels are explorations of motives, of decisions made under duress of war, plague, heartache, duty, honour and allegiance. The main theme of *The Green Popinjays* is finding a home – and for Lucia, that home was not in her ancestral bed, adorned by the emerald-eyed popinjays, but wherever she could dictate her own life, and have dominion over her own decisions – what any modern woman would want.

– *ELLA MICHELER, 2021*
SERIES EDITOR

AUTHOR'S NOTE

All the characters in this book were once living people. All events have a foundation in the history of Cleveland, but families have died out, documents have been destroyed, tombstones defaced. Only fiction can bridge the gaps.

The author wishes to acknowledge with grateful thanks the help given in research by Mrs G. R. Stainthorpe.

1

A shaft of early sunlight speared upward from the black trees, found the curtain wall of Kilton Castle and moved towards the narrow windows which faced east. Through these, it shone on a long, irregular-shaped room with four beds in it; three were bracken-covered wooden trestles, the fourth a carved and curtained dais.

Light leapt from the massive bedhead as soon as the sun touched it, because the three carved popinjays there had eyes of real emerald. Watching the burning green lay the Lady Lucia de Thweng, naked under a linen sheet. Blankets and a fur coverlet were bundled beyond the reach of her feet, like an animal, crouched. The April night had been warm.

'I intend to get up. Now. At once!'

She snapped her fingers at the birds and leapt out, as though pushed by an inner spring.

'I go riding with cousin Duke. I return to watch the games. I dress for the banquet…'

She spun around on her toes, holding the bed curtains. Emerald and red-gold and silver-grey, they wound her about in the armorial colours of the family de Thweng, and the popinjays' green eyes blinked rapidly from reflecting the movement.

Lucia began to dress with great speed. Pulling a sheep-skin shift over her head, leaning against the bed to don a pair of long, loose drawers. She tied the waist string. Now her thin body took on a bunchy appearance like an effigy in a church. A satin kirtle over the shift and drawers smoothed the outline, swelled the bosom, rounded the hips of her who was thin as a skinned rabbit. Over the kirtle, a dark green dress, satin also, so that one cloth flowed over the other, unresisting as water. The dress was tight-sleeved, loose-waisted, silver-embroidered around the wide neck which revealed the top of the kirtle. A heavy silver belt at the hips had her purse dangling from it, and a collection of medals and pilgrims' tokens that tinkled together when she moved.

Cross-gartered hose and flat-heeled pointed shoes completed her attire except for the heavy surcoat which she threw on the bed, ready to carry down with her.

Remained only her hair to be dressed.

'Perish it!' she muttered, dragging at it with a brush. It was thick, brown, heavy hair – 'like a ploughed field', her de Brus grandmother used to say of it. She always remem-bered the things her grandmother said and did.

There was the game with the carved birds, for instance. When the old lady occupied the ancestral bed in widowed solitude, the child, Lucia, would tiptoe into her room in the early mornings.

'Now, Granddaughter, what brings you here before cock-crow, eh?' The old lady never seemed to sleep.

'To see you, Granna, of course.'

'That is a great fat lie. You have come to watch the popinjays' eyes light up.'

Then Lucia would bounce on the bed with shrill laughter and, presently, the sun would pick out the little birds from among the crowded arms and emblems of the generations that had begotten this child. Grandmother de Brus could make the birds' eyes blink or shut or twinkle just by waving her fat jewelled hands, the jewels embedded in the flesh like the emeralds in the bedhead. She could make the green glow transfer itself to the white linen sheet. She could wrap the birds up in the fur coverlet. There was no end to the things Grandmother de Brus could do without lifting her back off the padded leather bed.

The laughter from the room would arouse the entire household in grumbling protest.

'I shall always be happy in this bed,' Lucia remembered saying once to the old lady.

'Will you, dearest? Just for that, I will leave it to you when I die.'

DEATH CAME to the carved bed when Lucia was just growing out of babyhood, and brought a vast change in her state. She was an heiress now twice over. Already an orphan, she was mistress of vast lands inherited from her parents. On the death of her de Brus grandmother, the forest of Danby in Cleveland became hers and a moiety of the Bailiwick of Langbaurgh. Her personal possessions ranged from fabulous jewellery to gold and silver tableware and chestfuls of clothing beautiful enough – and shapeless enough! – to be passed on from one generation to the next.

Slowly, the idea took root in her mind that, one day, she would have to go and live on one or other of her holdings. Weeping and terrified, she ran to her Aunt Isabel.

'Child, child,' Isabel comforted, 'you are not going

from Kilton. We are appointed your guardians, your Uncle Marmaduke and I. You are the King's ward.'

'I shall be here always, with my cousin Duke?'

Isabel looked over the child's head and her eyes were soft.

'I pray God so. You and my son. In Kilton.'

Duke was the eldest of the boy cousins; named after his father, he was always called by the shortened form of the word. Lucia was devoted to him and, after a while, he took a condescending form of interest in her welfare. She would wait patiently until he was freed from lessons, then roam the woods and moors with him while her girl cousins were bent over their needlework. She won his love by making her company indispensable to him. She had no other wiles so early.

Childhood slipped easily away and here she was now, fifteen already and almost a woman. The year was 1293.

She parted her heavy hair in the centre and brushed it, waist-length and loose, from a little fillet of enamelled flowers.

A burnished metal salver by the bed gave a passable reflection of her face: a high, rounded forehead, the hair-line uneven; long-lidded eyes; a wide mouth, the lips strongly defined. Not a face that conformed to the current ideal of beauty that hair should be 'yellow of hue' and eyes grey-blue. Lucia's eyes were brown, gold-flecked.

Grimacing, she put the salver down with a clatter, having no foreknowledge that the title 'Helen of Cleveland' would, one day, be hers.

One of her girl cousins, Catherine, sighed deeply from the next bed and turned over, with a rustle of bracken, to snore softly. The other two, Margaret and another Lucia, slept on without a sound.

The early riser threw her surcoat over her arm and tiptoed out of the room.

'No use in going to the tower apartment,' she decided. 'My aunt and uncle are as heavy headed in the morning as their daughters! I can pay my respects later.'

No use going to the private chapel, either. Friar Alan would be engrossed in meditation there, not ready to read Mass for another hour or more, and quietly resentful of anyone who would interrupt him so early. More hermit than friar, he divided his time between the chapel and his cramped apartments in the apsidal tower. His contact with the eleven youngsters of Kilton Castle – Lucia and her cousins, three girls, seven boys – lasted only during morning lessons.

Today there would be no lessons, not even for the two boys destined for Holy Orders. The forthcoming games and banquet overshadowed everything.

Lucia went along the passage under the rampart walk and into the Great Hall. Women were already at work there, strewing the floor with fresh rushes. The old floor-covering, down for a month and more, was piled in a corner, smelling of stale food, old tallow, dampness and dogs. There was no room more gay on a feasting night than the Great Hall of Kilton, and none more desolate and foul in the early morning.

Lucia ran down the stone steps to the ground floor. Here, bakery and store-rooms smelt sweet indeed. Through the open door of the kitchen nearby, she could see the glow of fires and the gleam of sweat on men's bodies as they worked at table and trough, shouting, cursing, singing, while the majestic figure of the chief cook presided. Vested with much authority, his was the glory of a dish that pleased, the shame of one that did not.

The Inner Ward, too, was a hive of activity. Crossing it

to the barbican gate, Lucia smiled secretly at the placidity of a youth patiently holding her horse. His must be the only idle body in Kilton this day except for the sleeping family! He waited thus every morning whether she wanted the horse or not. When ordered by the head groom to do other work, this one – who had red hair and vivid blue eyes that squinted alarmingly – would reply that he was ''tending to the Lady Lucia's mount'. For fear of Lucia's wrath, the head groom never pressed the matter further; he considered – wisely, as it happened – that the fury of a King's ward could be dangerous, especially when the King was Edward the First.

The cross-eyed youth cupped his hands and she put her foot lightly into them to mount.

Her horse clattered under the portcullis towards the Outer Ward. Here, labouring men drew aside to let her pass; they doffed their felt and woollen caps, bidding her good morning and God speed, and a few of the more romantically minded paused a while to look after her, the image of her bright face still in their minds. Her back was very straight as she rode away from them, flowing hair and surcoat like half-furled wings. She was smiling to herself with anticipation of meeting Duke, and her hair floated in rhythm with the horse's gait.

Behind the West Ditch now there was shouting and hammering. Wooden terraces were being erected for privileged onlookers of the games, and a blue silk pavilion was being drawn upwards on its ropes and pulleys, the material billowing like shallop sails.

She said to herself, 'I wish we could have a real tournament!' – but Kilton was too small, too unimportant. It had no lands to give away in prizes and its daughters were all under marrying age. Still, the list of competitors this year was impressive; there would be a little jousting and tilting as well as games and trials of skill.

Beyond the makeshift terraces now, she saw Duke's blue velvet cap bobbing up and down as he cantered about waiting for her – uncertain, as always, whether she would come or not. It pleased her to tease him, even to hurt him: yet she loved him with a double intensity, that of a sister-cousin and of spiritual mistress. And all his ideals were centred in her. She knew that.

They did not speak when they met, but a sidelong smile passed between them as they rode clear of the workmen and steadied their mounts, neck to neck.

'Aye, away!' Duke shouted.

They galloped northward to a point at the edge of the wood which (it had been agreed long ago) was the limit of the race. She could have beaten him this morning but chose not to do so. It was pleasanter to come second so that he could turn and stretch out a hand to steady her. Then he would keep his hand over hers as they rode forward again, slowly, deep into the wood.

'Where shall we go, Lucia?'

She knew what he wanted her to say, but pretended to give the matter much thought.

'The tide is out,' she said at last. 'Let us go down to the sea. We can ride along the sands, then inland to the church at Easington.'

He was very pleased. She felt his pleasure without looking at him, in a little tremor of his small womanish hand. The sand dunes beyond Huntcliff had a special significance for both of them. There was a certain spot where they had taken a solemn vow together never to return with anyone else if they were parted.

The vow was repeated in the tiny Norman church at Easington. They often attended the fishermen's Mass there, hearing the tinkle of the Consecration bell, feeling the nearness of each other without conscious gratitude for it because it had never been threatened. Lucia and Duke were destined for each other; their parents had arranged it; their own hearts demanded it. Only in the taking of the vow was any shadow of doubt implicit, the sudden doubt of fear that what is most beloved may be lost.

They had ridden far into the woods now and mist was still rising out of the marshy ground. Black trees slid silently past, the outlines of their trunks blurred, but, high up, new-leaved boughs caught the sunlight in waving plumes.

'Ghosts of Roman soldiers,' Duke laughed.

The mist blanketed his voice, cutting the words off with eerie suddenness. He reined his horse and signed to Lucia to draw in behind him: he was looking ahead and listening. She noticed the fog particles in his yellow hair and on the dark blue velvet of his cap. He had a jewelled appearance, like an imagined angel.

Almost at once, the dark shape of another rider came soundlessly out of the mist that hung, denser than else-where, over a pond of shallow, stagnant water.

'It's Peter!' Duke shouted. 'Peter de Mauley!'

He dismounted quickly and ran forward to greet his friend. But Lucia kept her seat rigidly, not wholly convinced that it was, indeed, the boy-Lord of Mulgrave. It was a year since she had seen de Mauley and he was then a child. Now, coming out of the wood's shadow, she had glimpsed his face, and it was not the face of a child but of a satyr. The contrast between his appearance and Duke's was as strong as the illustrations of Good and Evil in Friar Alan's manuscripts.

Apprehensively, she watched him come forward with Duke. Without a curtain of fog between her and them now,

Peter's skin appeared to be less sallow, his hair less black. She had been mistaken.

He paid his respects, looking up at her and smiling. He was almost a child again, except that his white teeth were very long and narrow.

'Good morning, Peter,' she replied, trying to remember that she was three years older than he was. 'Why are you riding all alone so early?'

His eyes mocked her attempt at matronly tones as their gaze travelled from the jewelled neckline of her dress down to the angle of her knee pressed against the horse's flank.

'I am not so lucky as Duke,' he said with deliberation. Then he turned away, bowing, to remount.

She was angry and shocked at his precocity, but bit her lip on a sharp reply. The families of Mulgrave and Kilton were friends. When she and Duke were married, it would be unwise to be on bad terms with de Mauley: feudal lords often had need of each other.

They rode on together, Peter retracing the path by which he had come. He had been on his way to Kilton, he said, for the games, but it was too early yet in any case. He wanted to talk to Duke, if my lady would pardon the intrusion.

My lady pardoned it with bad grace. She held herself aloof and remote from them while they discussed horses and a new fashion in armour. Her immediate concern was to analyse the cause of her intense anger with de Mauley. After all, reason argued, he had said nothing wrong. He had, in fact, paid her a compliment.

But he is too young, she told herself. *Too young to look as he did coming out of the trees – unless I imagined the resemblance to a satyr. Nevertheless, a boy of his age should not have looked at me as he did. His eyes are already those of a man who knows women.*

And now he was spoiling her morning with Duke.

Duke, boyish and excited, thinking only of the time when he too would be a knight like his father, was riding close to Peter, leaving a wide gap between himself and her on the other side. Bright spots of anger burned high on her cheeks and it was some time before she noticed that they had taken the wrong path for Easington. Nursing a spite against the two youths, so engrossed in each other's conversation, she decided to let them find out their mistake for themselves, but, after a while, said flatly:

'We're going the wrong way.'

'Oh?' Peter looked up. 'Where had you intended going?'

She did not answer him and Duke said, embarrassed:

'To – to Easington.'

'Easington? What for?'

'Well, there's a little church there. Lucia and I, we – we go to pray. When we miss Friar Alan's Mass at home.'

They sat their halted mounts and Peter de Mauley looked from Lucia to Duke and back again. It was difficult to read his expression – amusement, contempt, puzzlement, pity. Lucia threw back her head and stared at him. She felt the weight of her rich brown hair on her back and shoulders, and the heat of the angry colour in her cheeks; she felt, too, the eyes of both young men upon her and knew that she was desirable to both.

Peter asked very softly,

'What is it you pray for?'

She considered some wisps of straw on the left shoulder of his tunic, his generally unkempt appearance and his heavy-headed horse. Well, if he wished to consort with milk-maids, he was master of his own house…

'We pray for us,' she said, looking at Duke, 'that we may always be together.'

In the silence, Peter's laugh was shrill and sudden.

Lucia rounded on him, her grip fierce on whip and tasselled rein, but before she could reach him, he stopped laughing.

'Why not pray for something you have not rather than something which you have?' he enquired, composing his face into innocence. 'I always do.'

It was in that instant that she sensed the beginnings of a threat, not from de Mauley but from some intangible malignity which darkened the sun for her.

Nobody spoke. Then de Mauley slapped his tired horse and sent it scrambling up a bank.

'I'm for Kilton to watch the first contestants arrive,' he shouted from above. 'Good morning to my lady, and to you, Duke!'

Lucia watching him out of sight with the concentration of a wild cat.

'You should not have quarrelled with him,' Duke said earnestly. 'Kilton and Mulgrave have always—'

She did not hear him.

'I dislike the child,' she interrupted harshly, using the noun with a deliberate malice which was lost on Duke.

'Who, Peter? *Child?* Ha, ha. Oh, he knows more than both of us.' Duke led the horses back to the fork where they had gone astray.

'About what?'

'Er – heraldry and weapons and such. Even dull things like philosophy. He studies all the great pagans! He's a very talented musician, they say, and talks more wittily than a grown man. Why don't you like him, sweet?'

'I don't know,' she said slowly. 'Maybe, just now, because he turned your thoughts away from me.'

Duke stopped leading the horses and stood beside her, looking up at her. His arms encircled her knees and she felt the pressure of his body as he drew her from the saddle. They kissed with sudden fierce possessiveness.

'Come, my love,' he said softly, 'and see that no one can turn my thoughts from you.'

She left her surcoat lying across the saddle because the sunshine was warm now.

The horses began to graze as they wandered free in the stillness of the clearing.

2

As Lucia and Duke re-entered the Inner Ward, the eleven o'clock gong was already booming for the first meal of the day. They joined the throng converging on the Great Hall. Under cover of Lucia's green satin sleeve, their fingers touched and interlocked, making them a unit aloof from the hungry crowd that now milled on the stairs. Everyone, except this pair, was hilarious with anticipation of the day's sport and the night's feasting. But Duke and Lucia remained quiet within themselves, absorbed in the close memory of the sunny woods.

Catherine, one of Duke's sisters, was already at the dais table. Standing, she awaited the arrival of her father to say grace. Lucia took her place beside her.

'Lucia—' Catherine was dancing with excitement, '— Lucia, *so* many people are here already! Peter de Mauley, Guy Thornborrow, the Peacocks – yes, the entire family! – the brothers Fleming, the le Latimers... Oh!'

Catherine stopped dancing. She bit her lower lip and met Lucia's slow stare with a blink.

'What did you say just then?' Lucia whispered.

'The – the le Latimers. W-William and his father.'
Catherine was on the verge of tears now: she had been
warned not to tell…

Lucia had not recovered her voice.

'What do they want this time?' she whispered again.

Catherine shook her head dumbly. Now Duke leaned
across the table.

'What is it, Lucia? You look like the White Lady…'

'The le Latimers,' she said tonelessly. 'They're here.
Both of them. Pray excuse me to my aunt and uncle. I feel
ill.'

She stumbled back along the corridor where she had
walked so light-heartedly in the morning. *Le Latimer. Le
Latimer.* The name pounded in her head. *What do they want
this time? Something unpleasant. And of me. Always.*

She entered the deserted sleeping apartment, now a
litter of clothes and tumbled beds. She lay back on her
own pillow and drew the curtains tightly on all sides.

'I shall always be happy in this bed…'

Now she was afraid.

Outside, in the corridor, there were footsteps and
voices. She heard the great roar of Uncle Marmaduke's
laugh, the high trill of Aunt Isabel's. They were taking
their many guests down to breakfast. In a moment, all
would be quiet.

Then, just outside her door, Lucia heard another voice,
and she stopped her breathing for fear of being discovered
by its owner, the elder le Latimer.

The party moved away towards the Great Hall and she
relaxed. This sweating terror was unworthy and must be
conquered. They could do nothing to her now. She was no
longer a child. She would face them and defy them…

But not yet. Not this morning.

She lay in the dark, listening to the feeding clatter from

the Hall where noble, ignoble and dog shared the one roof. She was not hungry: there was a hard knot in her stomach. She tried to think of pleasant things, of Duke's words and kisses in the woods, but already these had a dream quality. The only reality was le Latimer's face hanging over her in the darkness. Inevitably, she relived their first meeting; it was her recurring punishment.

ALMOST A YEAR AGO NOW. She was fourteen. The fame of her inheritance had travelled far and already there were some who spoke of beauty in her face, although beauty was not exactly the word they sought: breeding, perhaps, or surging life behind the windows of her eyes. One de Thweng in every generation had this nameless quality since a Norman bishop had fathered the first of them.

At fourteen, Lucia was beginning to discover the extent, and the limitation, of her power as an heiress and a King's ward.

It was late autumn, already winter in Cleveland. After morning lessons with Friar Alan, her Uncle Marmaduke sent for Lucia in the tower apartment. There was a man with him there: middle-aged, hard and wrinkled, crooked-boned like a cur.

'Ah, Lucia, my pet' – her uncle seemed huge beside the stranger – 'this is William le Latimer, the Lord of Corby and Skenestone and a trustee of your estate. He has come to crave a favour of you.'

It had always been Lucia's instinct to like everyone on sight and to please them if possible. But for le Latimer she conceived a sudden loathing allied with a determination to thwart his every desire.

'Yes?' she regarded the stranger with hostility.

Marmaduke cleared his throat, embarrassed by her incivility.

'He – ah – he wants the tenancy of Kirkburn.'

'Kirkburn is occupied.'

'Only by a tied farmer.' It was le Latimer who spoke for the first time. His voice was dry as a stick. 'He must go if you say so.'

'I do not choose to say so.'

Marmaduke shifted his huge bulk uneasily.

'Come now, Lucia, there is more to this than meets the eye. You know I have trouble with Kirkburn in my administration on your behalf. Frankly, I think you would be well rid of this sub-tenant—'

She stared at him and his gaze dropped.

'Our guest here is willing to spend much on the buildings and the land.'

'I will not do it.' Normally, she acted without question on her uncle's advice and had never before thwarted him. Her faith in his judgement was implicit. Now, for the first time, she sensed that he was not speaking his mind, that he was being forced to utter false words.

Le Latimer smiled, showing yellow teeth.

'There is a higher authority,' he said ominously. 'I will not rush the lady into a decision. We will discuss the matter later in the day.'

When he was gone, she turned to her uncle who was staring into the fire.

'I – I am sorry…'

He aroused himself.

'I understand, Lucia. Tenants are like one's children. But, in this case, I beg of you to be guided by me.'

'Yet you are not happy about the matter?'

'No. I have never evicted a tenant in my life. Yet you must do it.'

'*Why?*' She shook him by the arm, feeling the bulk of him through the sleeve of his tunic. He disengaged her hand and clasped her around the waist.

'Lucia, what do you think of Edward, the King?'

'As a man? As a monarch? That he is strong, ruthless and will not be thwarted. Yet he is a great man and a great monarch. He has many vexations.'

'Yes. But in relation to yourself as his ward?'

'He is my supreme protector,' she said.

Marmaduke stirred, shifted a log closer to the blaze.

'The King owns you, Lucia,' he said quietly, 'and all your inheritance. It is to bestow where he will. His wards are his wealth and his surety for his debts.'

There was a long silence. She felt that she would never speak again, that there would be nothing to say, ever, for the foundations of her world were cracking, threatening to engulf her.

'It is – Edward – who gives Kirkburn – to le Latimer?' she whispered at last.

'Yes. In payment for services in the field.'

'Then I have no choice but to do as I am bidden?'

'It is best not to thwart the King, my love.'

'You mean, for a *woman* it is best? A man could take to outlawry in the forest, but a woman...' She became absorbed in some inner thought, and presently she smiled. 'A woman could be intractable, too, Uncle, if she were put to it and had spirit enough.'

'Not in this,' Marmaduke pleaded. Already, his niece had one minor rebellion behind her which had caused Kilton much discomfort – a refusal to agree with the Church over the matter of how much was owing to it from Lucia's estates... Somehow, Friar Alan had smoothed matters over, but there was a certain wariness now on all sides when dealing with Lucia, young as she was.

'I shall consider it,' she said airily.

At the meal that evening, she met the younger William le Latimer for the first time. Undersized, like his father, but tending to plumpness where the elder's bones showed through, his attire rather than his figure affronted her: he wore a stained and creased brown tunic laced untidily over a rough shirt. His fingers were blunt and grimed, his hair like the twigs in a raven's nest. Yet there was something about him which awoke a sympathy in her, although it may only have been the settled gloom of his expression.

She tried to talk to him as they ate. He replied in monosyllables, and that only after consideration. Defeated and depressed, she retired with the other ladies.

After a while, a servant came to summon her again to her uncle. Sudden anxiety gripped her: they would want her decision about Kirkburn, and she had hardly thought of it at all. She had intended talking to Duke about it, but he had not returned from hunting.

She entered the apartment, head high: the younger William lumbered to his feet, but le Latimer senior remained seated by the fire. Marmaduke was already standing. She thought he looked ill at ease and, for an instant, she was conscious of her great affection for him. By comparison with old le Latimer, he was a king, in manner and in stature, and she was proud of him.

'Lucia,' Marmaduke said, 'I now have further information about your tenant of Kirkburn, Walter de Rokesby. He is a very bad tenant indeed and is allowing the place to drift into desolation. Furthermore, he is insolent and will accept no message unless it be delivered by you, yourself in person.'

'Then he is safe for six months,' Lucia said grimly. 'The winter is upon us. A ride to Kirkburn now might take three days or three weeks depending on snow or ice or fog. It is sixty miles distant, with much moorland in between.'

'You make difficulties,' le Latimer said, peering over his shoulder from his crouched position by the fire. 'The weather is hard and dry, with bright sunshine daily. November is barely in. We could cover the moors in one day. I would advise my cousin, Thomas, at Sinnington, to lodge us that night. Next day, we could reach Kirkburn in an easy ride – it is level country – and return again to Sinnington Manor.'

Le Latimer spoke reasonably, almost soothingly. He even made it sound attractive – a trip in brilliant dry weather over the autumn-dyed moors, a last fling before the grip of winter tightened on Cleveland and a couple of nights as guest in a strange manor house! Well, well, such excitement was seldom offered at Kilton. And the journey would have to be made some time, in any case.

The purpose and the end she overlooked completely: that Walter de Rokesby, her sub-tenant, who had done her no harm except, perhaps, be a little backward with his work and a little careless over repairs to her buildings, was now to be evicted with his wife and child at the onset of winter.

'We will leave in the morning,' she said, 'there is still time tonight for preparation.'

THE DAY dawned jewel-bright with frost. Every sound was sharpened by the thin cold air, every line and colour intensified.

The party rode out with great clatter, and the entire household watched them go. First, Lucia, riding with her bailiff on her left, the younger William le Latimer on her right. Immediately behind followed the elder William, alone, sitting his horse like the experienced campaigner that he was. Then came four archers – two would ride ahead presently – two pack-horses and two attendants. Another servant had gone ahead overnight with a message for Sinnington.

Lucia's main feeling was one of importance. Without her, this party would not be: she was the only one really necessary. All eyes were upon her. Her hair was tightly bound. She was wearing the magnificent leather riding habit made for a de Brus four generations back. The blood pulsed in her neck with excitement and pride.

It was only when Kilton was far behind, and they were high on the desolate moors, that a thought forced itself to the surface of her mind.

What are you going to do at Kirkburn? What are you going to say to Walter de Rokesby? Are you, seriously, going to evict him at this time of year? Why did you not play harder for six months' grace for him?

She rode for some miles with her bailiff, discussing the matter earnestly with him. When she dismissed him, he joined the archers in front.

Now Lucia wished that she had asked her cousin Duke to forego the winter hunt for a few days to accompany her. The dying countryside depressed her. Everything spoke of winter's approach, of cold, of darkness, of probable hunger. She longed desperately to be back safe at Kilton, or to have Duke here with her, for the miles yawned ahead, up hill, down dale, into a vast greyness that was the November twilight.

She was not important here. She was an insect scrambling up one side of a furrow, down the other, without contact with any of her kind. Infinite loneliness possessed her and she rode close to the silent William.

Assured that his father was out of earshot, William surprised her by talking at some length: not with animation, to be sure, but with a certain weighty seriousness that impressed. A dull, sincere young man, she decided, plagued by a detestable parent. She was sorry for him. She even liked him a little and, for that very reason, could never love him.

As they drew near Sinnington and the leafless woods closed around them in the half-light, it became suddenly urgent to her to enlist William on her side.

'William, will you help me in this difficult business tomorrow?'

'As I may,' – glumly.

'Do you think it is right?'

'Yes,' he said then, sighing.

'Why?'

An even longer period of consideration.

'Because the overlords must push their authority with all their strength, while that lasts. Thus, they will gain a few extra years.'

'What do you mean, a few *years*?'

He shrugged.

'One day, the peasants will rise up and murder us all.'

She laughed outright, remembering all the homely, happy people who lived and worked at Kilton. Why, they did not even want their freedom…

SINNINGTON MANOR LOOMED up out of the trees and, presently, a hunchbacked servant came out to open the gates. There was no welcome in his eyes and he did not speak.

The party rode into the dark courtyard.

Now a door was flung open in the west wing of the

manor: light streamed forth and Thomas le Latimer came noisily to greet his guests. He was a fat man of middle years, very loud of voice.

'Greetings, my lady! Greetings, cousins! Come, come...'

He plunged about, called the hunchback a bastard, helped Lucia to dismount, then loaded himself with gear from the pack-horses and staggered towards the house, talking incessantly.

A pleasant meal was laid ready in a small apartment within and they ate in an intimate privacy which was very strange to Lucia after Kilton's Great Hall. Also, she found the scarcity of servants at Sinnington extremely odd.

'All buying their way out,' Thomas le Latimer told her, between bites on a mutton bone. 'Too much money. Wool, you understand. Foreigners will pay anything for it. Tenants sell wool, buy land. No holding them in another generation or two.'

Towards the end of the meal, she began to feel drowsy and paid little attention to the cousins' conversation until the matter of Kirkburn was broached. Thomas was surprisingly well informed about this affair and remarked that he was looking forward to the morrow.

'You are coming to Kirkburn with us?' Lucia enquired.

'But certainly, my lady. Young William here is not much support for you...' He thumped William between the shoulder blades and the young man choked on his wine.

Lucia's eyes narrowed on William's father.

'Where are *you* going tomorrow?' she demanded, wide awake.

'I have business in York.'

'Does my uncle know of this?'

'Your uncle accepted my word that you would be well

taken care of. Is it not enough that my cousin, Thomas, troubles himself to ride with you?'

Since she was under Thomas's roof, there was little protest she could make. She had no quarrel with Thomas – who now wore the expression of a large dog, unjustly kicked – so she begged his pardon for apparent ungraciousness, said that she was very tired and asked if she might retire.

A woman was summoned to escort her to a cold, triangular apartment. The woman was as silent as the hunchback at the gate had been and Lucia dismissed her before undressing. Afterwards, still in her shift and drawers, she lay shivering on a wretched palliasse covered by a mouldering fur and, in her mind, the fantasy of a gay adventure crumpled: this was the journey and the manor house and the company that had enticed her into leaving Kilton; remained only the unpleasant reality of the morrow.

THE PARTY ARRIVED at Kirkburn to find gates and doors barred before them and fields deserted, but it was not the desolation of withdrawal: the lowing and stamping of animals could be heard from within the barricaded stables and there was a blue wisp of smoke from the house vents.

'They defy us!' said Thomas, his voice subdued.

The horses moved uneasily.

Lucia looked up at the shuttered windows across the courtyard and she felt that eyes were watching through the chinks.

The absence of human noise at mid-afternoon on a farm was uncanny. Now, even the rowdy Thomas was stricken dumb by its impact.

Very well: Walter de Rokesby, the tenant, had been

warned of their coming, probably only that morning. No secret had been made of their purpose even before leaving Kilton. There were signs of haste about Walter's retreat; a child's wooden toy just inside the outer gate; a man's cap topping a rake that leaned against the wall; a milk pail outside the kitchen door.

Lucia dismounted, walked towards the gate and shook it, waited, rattled it again.

Within the manor, a dog barked, the sound ending abruptly as though a hand had been clamped around its muzzle.

The tension unnerved her and her voice was unnaturally high-pitched when she called to the archers:

'Break the gate down!'

The four of them fell upon it and it yielded.

It was against all her instincts to enter the silent courtyard. There was something here to be feared – not a rebellious tenant nor his stave-armed labourers, but something else, an atmosphere of brooding ill, like witchcraft and curses.

She rode forward slowly between the gaping gate that now sagged between stone pillars. Her horse stumbled and, looking down, she saw the wooden toy lying trodden.

They grouped in the courtyard and her bailiff took command at her signal. He shouted up at the blank windows. Nothing stirred. He thundered on the kitchen door.

'Open. We will break in…'

They waited. A child began to cry upstairs.

The bailiff signed to the archers and they set their weight to the stout door. They strained for a very long time and the child cried continuously. Finally, hands and voice shaking, Lucia turned to William.

'Help them! Have done with it quickly.'

He was advancing on the door when a shutter was torn from a window in the east wing and stones began to rain into the courtyard. Lucia's horse, hit in the neck, reared wildly and its frantic whinny set the other mounts in a panic.

Now other shutters were ripped away and every bared window emitted stones and jagged pieces of crockery, all thrown with great force.

The dismounted archers raced for their horses and the party retreated in confusion towards the broken gate. Lucia had lost control of her horse and was carried thither whether she wished it or not.

William, alone, stood in front of the kitchen door, heaving and battering against it with his shoulders while missiles rained upon him from above. He made no attempt to retreat, but whether through bravery or sheer oblivion to anything except the task in hand, no one ever decided. His terror-stricken horse had backed against the west wall and, from a window above, now descended a huge bundle of rags and bracken, one end already blazing, the other alight. This may have been a bed, fired accidentally and thrown out in haste before it could do any damage indoors, or it may have been a deliberate weapon. In either case, it was to wreak havoc.

Somehow, the trailing rein of William's horse became entangled in the fiery bundle. The horse fled madly towards the door of a stable opposite and began to pound the wood with reared hooves. Inside the stable, penned animals smelt smoke and went berserk. In an instant, the courtyard was filled with maddened beasts that broke all before them.

In the same instant, the door yielded to William's onslaught and he stumbled into the kitchen where he was set upon by two men.

Now the rest of the party reorganised at the gate. Most of the animals had streamed through, making for open country, running, stumbling, jostling, making the noises of their kind. Thomas charged the remainder to go to his cousin's aid.

It was a brief battle. William himself had overpowered the two men in the kitchen and only three more were found in the east wing. They were all labourers. Their attempt at defending Walter's rented manor had ended in greater loss for Walter than if they had left him to his fate.

Lucia's voice came sharply from the courtyard.

'Where is Walter de Rokesby?'

The labourers were frightened now, and anxious to appease her.

'Upstairs, lady. At the back. He—'

'That will do. I will go up.'

Now Thomas was agitated. Things had worked out badly enough under his leadership without anything happening to Lucia de Thweng.

'He may harm you—'

She rounded on him.

'Get out, all of you!'

She watched them retreat sullenly from the kitchen – William, Thomas, the labourers – and join her bailiff and the archers outside the door before she herself entered.

She looked around quickly. There was a scattered fire on the hearth. A dresser full of delph had fallen over during the struggle and broken crockery littered the floor. In the hearth corner, a carved cradle was rocking gently as though by ghostly hand. But the child above had ceased to wail.

She stooped under the low arch that led to the inner staircase and called upward into the dark:

'I am the Lady Lucia de Thweng. I require words with you, Walter de Rokesby.'

Nobody answered.

She ascended the stairs and it was a conscious act of courage to do so, not knowing what was to be faced. Perhaps a madman. And in the total darkness.

She thrust back the heavy curtain over a doorway at the top.

Inside the windowless apartment, a rushlight burned. A man was kneeling on the bare floor beside a tumbled bed. He did not turn to look at her. He was stroking the corn-coloured hair of a woman who lay on the bed, a baby in her arms, another child – a boy – curled up, asleep, in the bend of her knee, his face flushed and shiny from long weeping.

The man staggered to his feet. He seemed half-blind. Tall and thin, he stood swaying like a storm-wracked tree, his shadow from the rushlight rising and falling on the rough walls.

'My wife is dying,' was all he said.

Lucia ran to the bed and leaned over the fair-haired woman. There was no movement of breathing in her and her eyes were closed.

Lucia moved to lift the baby out of the mother's arms because she could see that the child was already dead. Instantly, the woman's eyes opened and burned into hers, fever-bright.

'Do not touch him!'

Hypnotised, Lucia remained bending over the bed, her hands outstretched. She knew that Walter's wife must have been delivered of the dead child less than two hours previously, and she knew also that it was not a full-term infant. The sequence of events appalled her.

'Forgive,' she pleaded, kneeling. The other child on the bed sobbed convulsively in his sleep.

'I curse you,' the mother whispered, 'I curse you, Lucia de Thweng, in all your sons!'

Walter came over from the doorway and drew Lucia aside. He had to lift her from her knees.

'Pay no heed,' he whispered. 'The infant's death has turned her mind.'

Lucia wondered numbly why Walter did not hate her and, afterwards, knew that his misery was too great for any other feeling to have place within him. He would only have strength for hatred later on...

She went down slowly to the kitchen. The men were gathered around the door.

'Set everything in here straight,' she ordered. 'Build up the fire. Release the labourers to go and fetch their wives: there is tending of sick and child here. And any man who will ride, let him search for the animals and bring them back.'

She unhooked the purse from her belt and left it on the window-ledge. It was filled with gold, but she was aware of the paltry recompense.

Thomas and her bailiff were standing behind her.

'The eviction?' they asked in unison.

She looked about her at the desolate room and out into the rock-strewn courtyard and over the stretches of land where neither man nor beast was to be seen.

'It is done,' she answered. And they did not dare question her, because her face bore an unforgettable expression.

3

Lucia awoke, shivering, in her big bed, and the darkness of the tightly drawn curtains confused her. She did not know for how long she had slept, if sleep it had been: the entire reliving of the Kirkburn journey had made her bones ache as though with saddle weariness. But there was no sound now from Kilton's Great Hall. Everyone had gone outside to the games. She could hear distant shouting and cheering.

When she drew the bed curtains, there was no longer sunlight in the room. Noon had passed.

She heard footsteps approaching along the corridor, quick steps accompanied by a jangling of trinkets.

'Aunt Isabel!' she called. '*Aunt Isabel...*'

As in a nightmare, she sought for a comforting presence.

The lady came quickly into the room, filling the air with the scent of her garments, making little noises with her tongue like a gathering of confused birds.

'Lucia – dear child, where have you been? Are you ill? We—'

'Aunt Isabel,' Lucia sobbed, and threw her arms around the astonished lady's neck, kneading the plump smoothness of the skin with frantic hands.

'Why are you crying?' Isabel wailed. 'I *knew* there was something wrong when we could not find you. Aha' – her brow cleared – 'you have quarrelled with Duke! Of course. Well, it will pass. Tonight, at the banquet—'

'I had a dream,' Lucia said, instantly composed. 'It stayed with me beyond waking.'

'Then there is no quarrel and you are not ill?' Isabel's relief was evident.

'There is nothing wrong, dear aunt, except an ache of the bones. Talk to me a while.'

'Well, I came in early from the field to make sure that the Hall was ready. Everything progresses. We must begin to dress soon. Duke will tell you about the prizes and the events, and the girls know everyone by first name and full title! You have much time to make up, niece. Tell me what you will wear.'

'I shall wear,' Lucia said with relish, 'my ivory gown sewn with pearls and my doeskin slippers. I shall wear the emerald-studded girdle which has a fillet to match and the big emerald ring of Grandmother de Brus.' She began to laugh and leapt off the bed, utterly forgetful of what had sent her hiding there in the first place. 'What will *you* wear, Aunt?'

'Oh dear,' Isabel fluttered her hands, one of her many helpless gestures, 'I shall wear whatever my daughters leave me!'

They laughed together, and Isabel thought how beautiful her niece was growing – more beautiful every day she spent with Duke. Could loveliness be taken away again, suddenly, from a human face, if the root of joy and love were destroyed? Watching her niece laugh, the Lady Isabel remembered why she herself was here: her husband had asked her to talk to Lucia – not to say too much, just to prepare the way for what he anticipated was going to be the most difficult task of his life.

'Lucia, my sweet…'

'Yes, Aunt?' She was trying on her emerald fillet, scooping up her hair through it and tossing it back.

'You … you know the le Latimers are here?'

'I do.' The smile left her face.

'Lucia, you like young William, don't you?'

'Well enough. Why?'

'Oh, nothing. No reason.' Isabel looped her yellow skirt over her arm and prepared to leave. Her niece gripped her firmly by the wrist.

'*Why?*'

'Lucia, that hurts – I told you: nothing.'

'You do not lie well, Aunt. Now tell me why the le Latimers are here. What do they want me to do this time? Murder another woman and her child? Send another man homeless into the winter?'

Isabel's light blue eyes filled with tears because her niece's fingernails were biting into her arm. Pain was abhorrent to Isabel, who had nevertheless borne ten children without complaint. But she considered any means of escape from other pain legitimate.

'They have come to ask you to marry young William.'

For an instant, it seemed merely another part of the nightmare to Lucia. Marriage – to William le Latimer…

She released Isabel's wrist and grasped the emerald fillet in both hands. It snapped across cleanly. She dropped both pieces on the floor and moved them with her foot.

'I will not do it,' she said.

And she remembered at once that those were the words

she had used concerning Kirkburn. But she had gone, and done what le Latimer asked.

Now the storm, which her uncle had feared, broke. As though possessed by a demon, Lucia confronted him, her hair wild, her dress crushed from sleeping in it.

'I will not do it,' she screamed. 'I will not!'

'Lucia, calm yourself. They come only to ask—'

'Only the King can compel. And, if he does, Lucia, is it so bad? I am not a rich man and my son who follows me will probably be a poor one. The King would not consider giving you to Duke.'

'Did you ask him?'

'No. I am not close to the King. And I thought there was plenty of time yet—'

Marmaduke, fumbling, procrastinating, humble: le Latimer, shrewd, land-hungry, a soldier of proven worth to the Crown. Lucia saw them both, standing together before her mind's eye, and she knew that she must be her own champion.

She sought out Friar Alan in the apsidal tower.

'Would you marry a woman who steadfastly refused to answer to the service at the alter?'

After two hours of conversation and argument, the Friar's views were clear to Lucia: a woman's will should be that of her parents or guardians. If it were otherwise, then she must be saved from herself by the imposition of a superior will upon her own. And Friar Alan would do as his Bishop ordered him.

Very well. She would ride and see the Bishop. Now, this instant, she would set out.

'That, my child,' said Friar Alan sadly, 'would be very unwise. My Lord Bishop is unlikely to be sympathetic to one who has already flouted his authority. Yes, the matter of the Church moneys which you refused to hand over...'

Now Lucia cursed as she had heard the stable men curse, and the good Friar put his fingers in his ears and went back to his prayers.

She decided to proceed more warily. No use acting like a madwoman when her adversary was the far-sighted le Latimer – the man who had business in York when he sensed trouble in Kirkburn!

She would dress. She would be quite beautiful. And reasonable. And adamant.

∿

THE BETROTHAL WAS ANNOUNCED at the end of the banquet, and, within a week, all arrangements completed for the wedding, which was to take place at the beginning of August.

Lucia's incredulity gave place to numb despair. Four months, that was to be the limit of her life at Kilton. Four months – with Duke… She walked about, dazed, as rebellion lost the battle within her to hopeless fatalism.

On the day of the le Latimers' departure from Kilton, Lucia made one final appeal, first to the elder, then to the younger.

Le Latimer senior's reply to her impassioned statement of the case was:

'The arrangements are made according to the King's order. Would you now make fools of us all?'

And she, who had humbled herself into pleading with him and into acknowledging her love for her cousin, now set her mouth in a firm line.

'Mayhap there is time for foolishness afterwards…'

But afterwards would be too late.

She saw her prospective bridegroom alone.

'William, I ask of you by the friendship you have shown me, what happiness can come of this?'

William regarded her from under lowered eyebrows, a habit he had which irritated her, reminding her of a tethered bull.

'A little – for me,' he said then, humbly.

As at their first meeting, irritation gave way to pity. But now, ruthlessly, she drove the gentler feeling out.

'I will break your heart,' she threatened.

He sighed. He demanded little from life, expected nothing. In the shared experience of his family, all marriages were doomed; this could be no worse than most.

He rode out of Kilton's gates with his father and turned once in the saddle to look again at Lucia. His abiding memory of her was to be that she was standing very close to Duke, their fingers interlocked within the satin folds of her sleeve.

Now, with the le Latimers gone, some of the oppression lifted from her mind. Sometimes, for an hour or two in in the early May sunshine, she forgot the brevity of her future at Kilton; but, always, she was called back to reality. There would be an altered dress to discuss; some questions of packing tableware to be settled; a sermon from Friar Alan on wifely duties. To all these things she attended scantily and often with bad grace. The Lady Isabel was frequently reduced to tears.

'Lucia, will you not help? I am dazed with planning food and wine towards August and attending all else besides!'

'Aunt, those who will have a circus at the price of my life are welcome to help. Let them polish every stone in the village church if they will. But I shall not even brush my hair on my wedding morning.'

Isabel sniffed and flapped her hands.

'You will have much attendance that day. Ah, I remember my wedding to your uncle——'

Lucia went down into the steep, sun-dappled woods between the castle and the river, and sat down to wait for Duke.

'You will have much attendance that day...' To what purpose? To make her more beautiful? They would bathe and scent her, dress and deck her, polish her hair with silk, and she would be the most highly prized bride to come out of Cleveland for a generation. How then to thwart them? Cut off her hair? Smash and burn and scatter her possessions? Scream defiance at the altar?

No.

She lay back on the warm grass, hearing the tinkle of water over sun-dried stones.

Le Latimer himself had given her the answer. *Make fools of us all...*

By God in the blue heaven above, she would do that and have the love she craved as well.

Duke came wading across the shallow river and she sat up, shading her eyes. Bright droplets of water fell from his bared thighs. His blue tunic was stained with rock moss and his white linen sleeves were pushed up almost to his shoulders. A lock of yellow hair clung wetly to his forehead where he had lain flat on a rock to catch a trout. He now waved the fish by the tail.

She lay back again on the bank and he flung himself down beside her, throwing the trout into the shade of a giant tree behind them. She was smiling.

'You look happy, my love,' he said, propping himself on his elbows.

'Because you are here.'

They kissed.

'Duke, do you love me?'

'With all my heart and forever.'

'Forever.' She looked up at the sky through the vaulted tree branches. 'In four months, I shall belong to William.'

'I have begged you not to say that—' He was very agitated.

'Does it make you angry, Duke? Does it make you feel robbed of what could be yours, now?'

She regarded him sidelong, saw the quick flush under the fair skin of face and neck.

'Does it make you wish that you were a man, a knight, able to battle for your rights?'

Gropingly, he replied:

'I am my father's squire. His battles are mine.'

She kissed him again, gently.

'You are my champion, my only love. Save me.'

'How?'

'By dishonour.'

He climbed slowly to his feet and walked down to the river. Unmoving, she watched him. After a long time, he came back and his eyes had the dedicated expression of a crusader's.

'I will come to you tonight,' he said, 'when my sisters are asleep.'

He picked up the trout and stood awkwardly holding it for a minute, then flung it back into the river, a silver arc piercing rings of bright water.

THE MOON WAS HIGH, remote, and the long room hazed in a blue-grey reflection of the sky.

Lucia's girl cousins lay sleeping. The last sounds died away inside the castle and out in the Wards, until only the deep surrounding woods were wakeful with the noises of the night creatures.

Duke entered so silently that Lucia did not hear him until he knelt by her bed. His clasped hands were extended, resting lightly on the rise of her hip under the coverlets. She saw the sheen of yellow hair on his bowed head, the whiteness of linen on his arms in the ghostly light from the window.

Clutching the covers high under her chin, she sat up, her back arched bare above the pillows because her hair was bound. He touched her arm and shoulder gently, awed by the softness of skin seldom uncovered.

'I touch heaven,' he whispered.

And, later:

'I hold heaven in my arms.'

THROUGH THE WARM nights of May and June the lovers continued their meetings and, in the cathedral of the summer woods, walked hand in hand. Too young in experience to disguise their passion, they yet found no one to denounce them nor bid them part: their time was short and the elders left them alone.

It was mid-July before le Latimer senior came, unattended, to see that all was in order for the August wedding. The prospective bridegroom had been ordered to stay at home, lest his company further infuriate Lucia.

She knew, early in the day, that le Latimer had come, and she sent him a message that she wished to see him privately, but not until after the evening meal. That would give him several hours in which to gloat over the possessions which he anticipated would come to his family after the wedding – gold and silver tableware, exquisite linen, furs, rugs and tapestries – as well as the lands and buildings which he had systematically visited since the betrothal.

Lucia smiled her tigress smile as she visualized him, counting the wealth of which he now hoped to be the sole administrator.

They met at the evening meal and he could not restrain himself from glancing sidelong at her several times as they ate.

'You look well, lady…' He noted the sun-browned skin, the burnished hair, the new fullness of her bosom.

'I am very happy,' she said demurely, and heard his sigh of relief with malicious amusement.

The interview took place in her Uncle Marmaduke's private apartment.

They were alone. Fully aware of her as a woman this time, le Latimer was courteous to the point of standing until bidden to be seated.

'You are reassured now, my dear lady, about the wisdom of this wedding?'

'Doubtless it was an admirable idea,' she replied, watching him intently. For a moment he had the sensation of being stalked.

'Ah,' he said then, relaxing.

She walked around him, soft-footed.

'My wealth for your high standing with the King,' she said.

'I prayed, Lucia, that you would see reason finally.'

She sat down, her back straight against the wall.

'Unfortunately, there are circumstances so undesirable from your point of view that wealth becomes meaningless.'

'I do not understand…' His tone was still placatory.

'You know that I love my cousin, Duke?'

Le Latimer spread his hands; this ground had been covered before, but he would not be impatient.

'Young love comes to all of us,' he said confidentially.

'I wish to marry my cousin.'

His control was breaking.

'This idea was put into your mind early, Lucia, by those who would keep your inheritance tied to Kilton.'

'You imply that my aunt and uncle deliberately fostered friendship and love between myself and Duke? You think that such a love as ours could be grown from the seeds of coercion?'

'I do not doubt the strength of your feelings, Daughter—'

'—Do not call me that!'

'Why? In another three weeks or so—'

'—You will be the laughing stock of Cleveland...'

They were both standing now, facing each other closely. For the first time, le Latimer saw the glowing flecks of amber in de Thweng eyes. Now the animal which had stalked him was about to spring.

'You had better explain,' he said quietly. Already, he knew the direction of the leap.

'I am with child this three-month by my cousin.'

A muscle twitched above the angle of his jaw.

'So you think there will be no wedding?'

'William would not—'

'William need not know. He is a fool in any case.'

She drew away from him, gathering her skirts from contact with the floor he trod.

'Animal,' she said. 'Foul, cunning, greedy, loveless fox... You would keep it from him until he marries me?'

'I would and I shall.' Le Latimer was relaxed again. He knew the enemy's position. Battle plans followed easily.

'I will tell him myself,' she shouted.

'It would make no difference: he does as I order. But, in

any event, you will be given no opportunity. You will not
see William until you walk towards him at the altar.'

Le Latimer prepared to leave. He paused at the door.

'The wedding must now take place here, in the private
chapel of St. Peter. We cannot expose you to prying village
eyes. I shall make the necessary changes.'

He bowed slightly and left her alone.

THE PRIVATE CHAPEL at Kilton was small but beautifully
appointed. East-lighted by three tall, slender windows
behind the white marble altar, its walls hung with silver-
grey and gold cloth, it had been witness to many a de
Thweng undertaking. Here, soldiers had prayed before
setting out to battle; Te Deums had been sung for victorious returns, and requiems of the dead... Lucia herself
was baptised in St. Peter's, where, within the year, both of
her young parents were to lie before their burial.

Now she was to be married here.

The windows blazed like torches in the August
sunshine. Guests in their wedding finery crammed the
carved benches: many, for whom there was no room inside,
sat or stood about in the corridors, waiting for a glimpse of
the bride.

It was whispered that all was not well with Lucia. She
had been abed for almost three weeks after a bout of sick-
ness and fainting. Therefore, the ceremony of the bride
bath had been curtailed, Isabel herself electing to prepare
the child in privacy. A few of the older female relatives had
grumbled loudly, but Isabel, for once, stood firm against all
entreaty and bribery.

A gong boomed in the Great Hall. The crowd in the
corridor pressed themselves against the walls to allow the

procession to enter the chapel: first, twelve acolytes bearing lighted tapers; then Friar Alan with a gold crucifix; he was followed by a choir, and that by flower-bearers; afterwards, with stately tread, the Lord Bishop and his retinue; then William, the bridegroom, suitably attired for once but heavy-treaded, slouch-backed like a felon going to the scaffold; his best man, a pace behind, acknowledged the murmured greetings of the guests on William's behalf.

It seemed that the little chapel would never hold this new multitude (the procession had been planned for the village church and the Lord Bishop was ill pleased with the change, but had given his word to solemnise the marriage in return for certain considerations), yet there was room for all, if not comfort.

Now the bridesmaids began their short journey to St. Peter's. They were Lucia's three cousins from Kilton, and for other relatives who had come a long journey for the honour. They all tried to outdo each other in decorum, but young eyes found the downcast position difficult and there was an occasional explosive giggle as they waited for Lucia.

A long a-a-ah sound passed through the crowd, mingled with the slow swish of silk as the bride approached. She seemed very tall in the straight ivory dress. A wine-red cloak curved from her shoulders like wings, the miniver tips held by pages, and her hair followed the line of the cloak to below waist level. It was the last time she would ever wear her hair unbound in public. She wore a fillet of fresh yellow roses, but not a single jewel on neck or hand or ear.

Aunt Isabel walked very close to Lucia, as though shielding her from the crowd with her own plump body and her hand constantly touched the bride's arm, guiding her. A stranger might have imagined that Lucia was blind.

The choir sang:

'Jubilate! Jubilate Deo…'

At the door of the chapel, Lucia looked up. She saw the three blazing windows, the sea of bobbing heads, the heavy magnificence of the Bishop before the white lace-covered altar. Then she saw William, standing alone, head bowed. Of Duke there was no sign. Her uncle now drew her hand through his arm and walked with her to the altar. She had no sensation of movement by her own will, but only of being propelled, inert and – at last – uncaring. The heat and the fierce brightness ringed everything with fire.

'Who gives this woman?'

'Dost thou take her?'

The bargain was struck.

'Deo Gratias!' the choir burst forth.

THE DAY's feasting and rejoicing was almost done and the time come for the bride to be escorted to her chamber, there to be joined by her husband. But a strange reticence had descended upon the company. They had observed Lucia throughout the long meal; she had eaten nothing; her face was ashen and no word or look had passed between her and William where they sat together in the places of honour at the dais table. How could one indulge in joyous jostling for the sport of undressing such a bride and putting her to bed?

Almost silently, they accompanied her to the door of the chamber where she had slept so long with her cousins.

She turned and faced them.

'Leave me. Go back to the Great Hall.'

They trooped away, not looking at her.

She stood by the unshuttered window, seeing the first stars reflected in the river far below. There was the spot where Duke had thrown the fish, there the bank were they had lain behind the giant tree; and, beyond the river, a path rose up steeply, white against the darkness of the undergrowth; that path led to all the places they had loved…

Tears tightened her throat. She turned towards the bed, remembering every night since the first time he had come to her; and she knew that her grandmother's shade was exorcised forever, taking with it the words of childhood:

'I shall always be happy in this bed.'

Through her tears she saw the twilight-dimmed popinjays, blurred and distorted, their eyes dead.

The door opened fumblingly and William came into the room. His wedding clothes were crumpled and stained with wine, his hair dishevelled.

Outside, in the corridor, men were laughing and shouting. William chained the door from the inside and the men went away.

He walked unsteadily towards Lucia.

'Do not touch me,' she said, very low.

He shook a lock of hair out of his eyes like a dog emerging from water.

'You are my wife—'

For a moment it seemed as though he would strike her, take her by force. Had he done so, she might yet have been his. Instead, he looked at her intently. It was nearly dark but he saw the hardness of her face, sensed the rigidity of her body.

'Go away,' she said, exhausted. 'In six months' time I am to bear a child to my cousin.'

For an instant, he was quite sober, then stupor worse than the first overcame him. His shoulders hunched, the hair fell again into his eyes. He shambled to the far end of the room and threw himself upon the girls' piled-up palliasses.

What he felt or thought she never knew. The night went by without sound or movement from the wretched corner where the heiress's bridegroom lay – a man whose wife had promised to break his heart.

4

At dawn, the pack-horses were brought out, heavily laden. Wagons followed, and mounted retainers. Twenty archers acted as outriders, constantly circling the rich caravan and sending scouts ahead.

Lucia saw the dawnlight beyond the narrow window and heard the clatter and rumble of horse and wheel leaving the Outer Ward, taking everything she owned away from Kilton.

She arose and dressed, her movements deliberate. When she was ready, she flung aside the shielding bed-curtains and called:

'William, get up at once!'

He obeyed her silently.

She prepared to leave the room, casting a cold glance over the wine-stained crumpled shirt in which he had lain.

'I will see that fresh linen is brought to you.'

She mustered a few servants in the Great Hall, some more around the kitchens and Inner Ward. The others were still at the barbican, cheering the wagons on their way.

All were astonished at the sight of the new bride, alone, so early. They were uneasy at the tone of her commands; her voice was harsh and there was no tenderness in the set of her mouth. Her garments bore none of the fripperies with which a bride is wont to adorn herself. Here was a wife who took up her duties too soon, too grimly.

She had the entire bridal party aroused by sun-up and a travellers' meal served for them for which nobody had a stomach. Everyone grumbled, heavy-headed, at the early start to a hard day's riding.

Isabel assembled her children and fussed over Lucia, but her niece was withdrawn from her, utterly remote and, in her farewell, almost formal.

'Goodbye, my cousin Catherine. Doubtless you too will be married when we meet again. Goodbye, Margaret and Lucia.' She kissed them all quickly and turned away. Her boy cousins filed past, all except Duke: of him there had been no sign since before the wedding ceremony.

'Aunt Isabel – dear mother, goodbye.' Isabel was weeping, but Lucia's eyes were hard and dry; she would weep later, and longer, for Isabel.

'Uncle Marmaduke...' She held out both her hands to him and he grasped them tightly, gave her a little shake and mumbled:

'If all is not well – come back to us!'

The mounted party passed under the barbican, while all Kilton cheered and cried:

'God speed!'

They galloped past the West Ditch, heading for the open moors to catch up with the wagons and the protecting archers. Among the trees beyond the Ditch, Duke watched alone and waved his private farewell to Lucia's straight back.

It was early evening when the wedding party reached Sinnington Manor. Then Lucia had the feeling of having lived through every event once already, from the moment when Thomas le Latimer emerged, shouting his greetings; except that a much larger company sat down to eat, nothing was changed. She knew that she and William would share the triangular room, that she would be utterly miserable and homesick, and that, on the morrow, they would ride on Kirkburn as before.

And so it was.

The bridal party was still almost intact, only a few members having left for their own homes. The rest were determined to see William and his bride settled in a permanent abode with their possessions unpacked around them. They were not to know that Kirkburn was occupied again by the widower, Walter de Rokesby. They were not to know that le Latimer senior was forcing his son and daughter-in-law to take up residence there because it was that part of Lucia's estate furthest from Kilton.

The party that rode on Kirkburn next day from Sinnington was merry and full of high spirits, the wine-heaviness of the wedding feast being now replaced by the exhilaration of moorland air.

There was general astonishment when the manor gates were found to be locked against their approach. Lucia, William and Thomas had dropped behind on the journey, sensing what was in store, so that the guests acted on their own initiative. They promptly broke the gates down and thundered into the courtyard with great uproar.

Immediately, they were set upon by an armed group, led by a tall gaunt man. Outraged, the wedding guests fought fiercely and called up the archers. The archers' weapons, however, were useless at such a short range, so that the intruders had little advantage over Walter de Rokesby and his labourers.

A pitched battle now developed in the courtyard, and damage to the manor itself and to the outbuildings was extensive. Blood flowed on both sides among the combatants. Finally, Walter de Rokesby and his followers elected to flee, outnumbered.

This was Walter's second eviction inside twelve months.

Now, at last, the pack-horses and wagons could enter the courtyard unmolested, their long journey over. Servants from Kilton and Sinnington swarmed over the manor, throwing out Walter's possessions and installing those of the newly-married couple. Food was unpacked and cooked. A great meal was served for guests and retainers in Kirkburn's lovely Hall.

'William and Lucia!' they toasted. 'Long life and happiness together. Many children…'

But Lucia heard only the ghost-voice of Walter's dying wife:

'I curse you… in your sons.'

The child within her stirred for the first time, and she prayed God for a girl.

Towards nightfall, many of the guests departed and, next day and the day following, the temporary servants returned to their old homes. The manor was then staffed almost entirely by local labour, strangers to Lucia.

She busied herself with many duties, setting out her own belongings as they had stood at Kilton.

Women were engaged to prepare clothing for the expected infant as soon as this might be done without comment. There was no one at Kirkburn now to remember how slim Lucia had once been.

William was away most days, laying in winter stores of meat and fuel, seeing to the lands and beasts of the manor.

By the end of October, a slight warmth as of home had begun to pervade the place for Lucia. There was routine, security, peace here. William did not interfere with her in any way and, at times, she felt almost friendly towards him. This was especially so when, of his own accord, he closed up the room where Walter's wife had died; Lucia was grateful for that act.

Now her industry began to wane as she grew bigger with the child. She walked more slowly, seldom asked for her horse to be brought out, and became short of breath after any exertion. The idea occurred to her that this was a preview of old age and she examined its every aspect with a kind of probing fear, but impersonally, as though it were some other woman who was growing old and heavy and slow, not Lucia de Thweng le Latimer.

On the sixteenth of November, the cocoon of peace and security with which she had surrounded herself was rent by the arrival of a messenger on horseback. William was presiding at a local court so that Lucia received the rider alone. He bore a writ, signed by the King himself, restoring the tenancy of Kirkburn Manor to Walter de Rokesby and ordering William le Latimer junior and his entire household to vacate the property without delay.

'Not now,' Lucia whispered, 'not at the beginning of winter…'

But the messenger only bowed his head over the document and bade her farewell. She remembered then that it was almost a year to the day when she herself ordered Walter and his wife to leave, with their little son and their unborn child. That day had marked the beginning of a curse upon her.

She summoned her husband home and, together, they

examined the writ. Lucia was frightened, as much by superstition as by the ominous wording of the document, and suddenly burst into hysterical weeping, clinging to William.

'Where shall we go? What shall we do? William, *William...*'

He made a quick review of their property and decided that there was only one roof of which they could obtain possession without dispute – that of the damp and dreary fortress of Castleton, long uninhabited except by rats from the River Esk.

'Oh God,' Lucia moaned. 'William, stay with me. I am so lonely. William – love me!'

He looked at her for a long moment. She was very beautiful, even in pregnancy.

'I will see that we move to Castleton with the least disturbance for you,' he said, and went out.

She never asked her husband again for a sign of love, or even of friendship. The fear of rebuff, deeply entrenched in both their hearts, now rose as a wall between them.

During the short bitter days of November, when freezing mists rolled down from the moors, the move was made from Kirkburn to Castleton, whose last occupant had been Lucia's own grandfather at the time of her parents' marriage; the old man had moved reluctantly out of Kilton so that Robert and Matilda might raise a family there, unhampered by his company. But alas! For the little girl-wife, Matilda: married at eight, a mother at fifteen and a corpse the same year – she lived long enough only to name her baby Lucia and to see the fortress of Castleton kill an old man with its dampness, its river mists and its rat bites.

'Have it destroyed,' Matilda begged. 'It is not fit for human habitation…'

Sixteen years later, it was still standing.

Kirkburn's winter stores of fuel, meat and grain, so carefully preserved at the manor, were now loaded haphazardly on wagons and sent out with only a few servants to guard them. One entire load was set upon by outlaws and stolen; the servants reached Castleton on foot, half-dead with hunger and cold after three nights on the moors. Another wagon overturned while descending a frozen hill track; grain was spilled and wine-casks broken.

William had arranged for Lucia to travel under cover, but, in her new defiance of him, she insisted on making the journey on horseback. She rode out of Kirkburn in the teeth of the year's first blizzard, cursing Walter de Rokesby, the King, her father-in-law and her husband collectively and singly. Huddled in her leather riding coat, feet and hands numb with cold, she reached Castleton in a state of near collapse.

No comfort awaited her in the fortress. Clouds of greenish smoke resulted from the servants' attempts at fire-lighting with wet wood. Food was scarce. Most of the inner walls were slime-covered and trickling. Rats ran along the dangerously rotten beams.

Such misery Lucia had never known.

The snow fell relentlessly, walling in the entire household with their animals.

Lucia took to her bed and tried not to think of giving birth to a child. Fiercely, she resented her state and the events which had led to it. The spring and summer at Kilton were now remote as a dream to her.

That night she was in a fever. Her mind had recoiled entirely from the dreadful present and she wandered along paths in sunshine, loved and familiar. Near death, she found happiness. While the household hovered about her and watched, she lay unmoving except for an occasional smile. Her delirium lasted for three weeks.

During that time, William had sent word to his father to come, for he wished to consult with him whether the de Thwengs should be summoned also. It had been their intention to keep Lucia and her family apart at all costs.

'I think not,' the elder le Latimer said after consideration. 'If she dies, it is as a result of their son's child, due in February. The de Thwengs cannot blame us for that.'

But on a morning in December, Lucia awoke to full consciousness with the pain of green apples eaten in haste. The child, a boy, was born prematurely, a weak and sickly infant, no more resembling his young parents than a day-old kitten resembles a tigress and her mate.

'A boy?' Lucia gasped, hopelessly.

'Yes, lady.'

'Then I am accursed forever.'

Now her father-in-law was truly incensed. Had she borne a full-term infant in the following February, it might somehow, have passed as the legitimate offspring of her husband. But a seven-month child could be nothing except a bastard.

Le Latimer's rage, however, was short-lived. He soon devised a method of turning the whole affair to his own great advantage, and summoned his cousin, Thomas, to Castleton, to discuss the plan with him.

'I tell you, Thomas,' he confided, 'this is the flowering of a dream, long planted in my mind. Ride up towards the moors with me, through the Forest of Danby, and I will show you a hill and build a castle in the sky before your eyes.'

It was a hard, bright, January morning. Bare trees were etched against a brilliant blue sky. The snow-whiteness dazzled the eyes of the two riders and the wind from the North Sea froze their breaths.

'Here,' William senior said at last, panting. 'This is the place. Look around you.'

A rolling vastness of forest and pastureland spread out to east and north and west. Southward rose a wooded hill.

'Here I will build a castle for my old age!'

'B-but how? This is de Brus land.'

'This is part of my son's wife's inheritance under the de Brus partition. She has been a bad bargain, Thomas, for all her wealth. Her son is, without any doubt now, a bastard of young Marmaduke de Thweng. How do you think the King will regard this? Will he consider her now ample reward for our services to him? I think not. I think he will make atonement to me, as head of the family, by granting me this favour: the Forest of Danby for life. And here I will build my castle to the best and newest plan yet seen in England. Listen…'

While the riders sat, frozen in a cloud of their own breathing, placing walls and towers, apartments and corridors, the child who was to make the building possible was being placed at his mother's breast. She scanned his face earnestly, seeking the image of Duke and not finding it. The child was fair-haired, fair-skinned, with a rare delicacy, but there was no other resemblance to any member of the de Thweng family. He was weak and listless. His constant wailing unnerved his mother, so that she became unable to feed him. A village woman, with a young child of her own still suckling, had to be found. And to her Lucia gave over the entire care of the infant.

In due course he was christened William, and was known as a le Latimer in spite of all evidence to the contrary.

Lucia's father-in-law now pushed his claims with the

King and made great play of having been deceived in his
son's marriage bargain. As a result of this, he obtained the
lordship and Forest of Danby for life; also a writ giving his
son seisin of all lands coming to the de Thwengs through
the de Brus partition of 1271.

Eight years later, in 1302, the building of Danby Castle
was completed, its outer West Wall showing the water
bougets of de Roos and the five escallop shells of le
Latimer. But of the de Thweng popinjays there was no
sign... Lucia never set foot in the Castle of Danby.

She regained her strength slowly after the birth of her
son. The comforting plumpness of motherhood hardly
survived her confinement and there was as little maturity
about her body as a year previously; thin and pale from the
terrible winter on poor food, she had little joy in being free
from the burden of the child's weight. She went about her
fortress home like a ghost, uncherished by her husband,
reviled by the other le Latimers and their friends for having
brought shame upon the family, albeit to that family's
benefit. Even her son did not need her; the primal bond
between them was never forged.

She would sit, sometimes, watching the baby's hands
feebly kneading the breasts of the nurse who fed him, and
she would remember Duke's hands on her horse's rein,
Duke stroking her thick brown hair, Duke holding the
bright fish up out of the sunny water... But she no longer
remembered that the infant was Duke's son: he was a le
Latimer by environment.

In March and April she began to take short rides
around the countryside in the company of a page,
Bartholomew de Fanacourt, a gentle foreign youth whom
she knew had been instructed not to allow her to go near
Kilton.

'Bartholomew,' she asked him one day, when they

stopped to gather white anemones in a little wood, 'are you happy as a page to my father-in-law?'

He blushed as easily as Duke used to do.

'Y-yes, my lady.'

'Do you miss your own home in France?' She looked away wistfully through the trees; over there must lie Kilton.

'Sometimes, my lady.'

'I miss mine,' she said.

Half-stooped over a clump of primroses, he regarded her in astonishment. It had never occurred to him before that Castleton was not her home. Now he saw the significance of the injunction against Kilton.

He arranged primroses and anemones carefully within a garland of spiked leaves and placed them in her lap.

'I am truly sorry,' he said. Close to, the fragility and pathos of her took him unawares. She was barely sixteen. Motherhood had come to her, and gone, leaving her undeveloped, unfulfilled. She, the Lady of Castleton, was more a child than he, the page of her household.

He regarded her steadily. Thin April sunshine picked out the gold flecks in her eyes and gave her a depth of colour to her heavy hair.

'My heart turns to Kilton every sunrise,' she said. 'I could ride there if I wished – you could not stop me, Bartholomew. But, because of you, I do not go. I have seen your cheek red and swollen before now by a blow from le Latimer. Oh, why do you not run away?'

His jaw muscles tightened.

'Because I want to be a knight, my lady, and I must serve my squirehood first. I do not fear a stroke on the cheek nor a whip on the shoulders. I will bear them gladly for you. Go to Kilton, my lady.'

It was the first word of friendship she had heard in many months. She began to cry.

But she never went to Kilton from Castleton, and, after that day in the little wood, she deliberately rode in the opposite direction, thus forfeiting her dream of meeting Duke somewhere between the two castles. Bartholomew, the gentle page, was made a squire that summer, but would still have to pay dearly for any time she spent with her cousin and lover.

By the end of April, when the baby William was five months old, his backwardness was apparent to all. With prematurity still almost halving his age, he was weak even for a three-month infant: his eyes hardly followed movement and his fingers did not grip. These things began to worry William, his father by adoption. For longer hours every day, the man would bend over the prostrate child in its crib, talking to it, trying to play with it, wishing strength into its blue-mottled body, recognition into its eyes. The child's development became an obsession with William. He neglected his hunting. He ceased to harry his tenants for due service and arms-bearing. He carried the child about for long periods in his arms while the nurse fretted for her charge's safety; William, though gentle, was uncommonly awkward.

Finally, however, it was le Latimer the elder who took his son to task, using as always the oblique barb.

'What do you suppose your wife does while you moon over her bastard?' he enquired, picking his teeth.

'She – she rides over the moors since the snow cleared.'

'I think not.'

'What do you mean?'

'I think she rides towards Kilton. The French de Fanacourt, whom I charged to prevent her doing that, swears that such is not the case – of course, to save his own skin. I place no reliance on him. He is too fond of her.'

The father watched his son narrowly. Surely there must

be some emotion called forth by this double doubt? But William junior only shrugged vaguely and scraped a stain off his tunic.

His father struck him, suddenly and savagely, on the head.

'Is it nothing to you, you fool, that she may bear de Thweng another child?'

William was silent and motionless now, the stain having responded to his thumbnail. The elder continued, talking almost to himself:

'You must leave Castleton. The wretched affair of Rokesby and Kirkburn is settled at last; gratefully he has taken the compensation ordered by the court and paid by us. He has departed to a more peaceful lodging. The manor now stands empty. Let you return there. Put at least two days' journey between your wife and her lover.'

He eased himself up from the bench and his joints creaked audibly. He grunted with pain and anger. Senility was anathema to him. He was a soldier, a builder, a planner. If he struck his servants more frequently of late, it was because his mind was occupied with architecture and not because he was an old man.

'All the same,' he said aloud, 'I'll leave you Bartholomew de Fanacourt. I have little time for soldiering now. *You* make a knight of him!'

Laughing uproariously, he went out to supervise his son's neglected duties and presently almost choked with rage at the extent of this neglect. The same day, he himself announced the removal of the household back to Kirkburn.

So, once again, the wagons were loaded and the fortress of Castleton left to the river rats alone.

5

Now, for the first time, the wars of England and the great national policies of her King, Edward the First, touched Lucia's life – which, later, was to be shaped almost entirely by these things. There was trouble with Gascony. An army was ready to be shipped under three commanders, one of whom was Lucia's father-in-law.

She bade farewell to this relative in the earnest hope that he might never return. His absence, however, brought many matters to a head.

Summertime came and went in the countryside around Kirkburn Manor. The marriage of William and Lucia was now a year old and they were more completely strangers to one another than at the outset; but it was the child, on whom William doted, who finally severed the union.

Many local servants engaged during the residence at Castleton had elected to follow the le Latimer household to Kirkburn. Of these, Mary Godwin, the infant's nurse, was one. She was a plump, smooth-faced woman, imperturbable, low voiced, quiet of movement, herself twice a mother and now a widow. The hours that William spent with the baby were spent perforce also in her company. To her he looked for confirmation of every new detail noted in his adopted son's development. From her strong arms he often lifted the child, his hands brushing her breasts as he did so.

It was during the summer of le Latimer senior's absence that William took Mary Godwin as his mistress.

Together with the infant, they now formed a family group from which Lucia was totally excluded; her authority within the household waned as soon as the state of affairs became common knowledge, for her husband had no delicacy in such matters. Finally, Lucia's contact with her son was broken except for a brief visit morning and evening.

She realised, too late, that things could never have come to such a pass while her father-in-law supervised the household, and, in her loneliness, she almost wished for his return; out of that loneliness was born her friendship for the little French squire, Bartholomew de Fanacourt, and it was this friendship that made possible the fantastic flight of Lucia le Latimer from her husband and Kirkburn Manor...

At first, she had not intended to implicate the squire. In her tenderness for him she feared his punishment. But, as autumn fired the woods and the weather sharpened and the days grew short, she knew that she had delayed too long to travel alone over wild moorland. She needed Bartholomew.

They were riding together towards Kirkburn on an October evening when the smell of leaves was sharp in the blue-misted air.

'Bartholomew, do you think the weather will hold good for another two days?' she tried to keep the anxiety out of her voice and yet to convey to him a subtlety of meaning in the question.

He looked at the flushed sky and the long, quiet, grey clouds spangled with early stars.

'For two days only, my lady,' he said then with mature certainty; hesitated, and went on, 'The nights will be bitter on the high moors.'

They reined their mounts and regarded one another levelly.

'You know that I am returning to Kilton Castle?'

'I have known for a long time that you would do so.'

'I need a horse. Tonight.'

'It will be waiting at this spot.' He snapped a branch from a tree, tied his handkerchief to it and threw the branch, lance-like, into the ditch. 'I too,' he said, facing her again.

They rode towards the dark manor.

Their plans were hasty, meagre and pathetic in their ineffectiveness against distance and weather, accident, pursuit and vengeance. But the blood that pulsed in both these young one's veins was an essence of two strong old families, and it had the essentials of survival in it.

Because William no longer slept in Lucia's bed, she knew that her absence would not be discovered until morning.

After the evening meal, she went up to see her son. Mary Godwin had finished feeding him and handed him silently, resentfully, to Lucia before going out of the firelit room and leaving them together.

Tonight, for the first time, the child seemed pleased to recognise his mother. His grip on her finger was tight and a strange feeling came upon her – a fierce, possessive love for him which she had not experienced before; an agony of protectiveness. She looked around the room while holding him upright against her shoulder; his clothing was scattered on the floor, his toys bundled on to a little chair. The sweet smell of his skin was in her nostrils and his small feet stamped rhythmically on her knee like a kitten's. She began to weep over the child and it seemed to her that a voice out of the past mocked her from every wall:

'*I curse you in your sons…*'

She laid him in his cradle and his arms stretched upwards towards her face. Tears blinded her.

'Goodbye, little William. You will never see me again, nor I you.'

She drew away from him and went out of the room without looking back. She heard him cry out, but it was Mary Godwin who went to comfort him.

She took her leather coat and a small bundle of belongings and flung them as far as she could out of the window of her apartment, noting the place where they fell. Then, casually, a woollen shawl about her shoulders, she walked down into the cobbled yard by the outer stair.

There was still much activity around the kitchens and out-buildings where lights flared in the October darkness. No one noticed her. She walked towards the gates, trying not to hurry, although it was necessary for her to pass through before they were barred for the night, or her return would be awaited.

Somewhere near, a man was talking, rattling keys as he did so. He was not standing near enough to the gates to notice her. She went out quietly onto the dark roadway which was deeply grooved with wheel tracks, and began to walk along, following the line of the manor walls, looking upwards to locate her own window. There it was, next to the child's room where the glow of the fire showed through slits in the shutters.

'Goodbye, William, my son and Duke's.'

She found the bundle and the coat in long wet grass. Already her skirt and shoes were saturated. She began to walk away from Kirkburn, shouldering her few possessions like a beggar maid. The stars overhead were frosty and there was no moon.

She found the lance-like branch with the handkerchief impaled upon it. Nearby, she heard the champing of horses.

'Bartholomew?'

'Yes, my lady. I heard your approach but dared not startle you.'

He took the leather coat from her and fastened it around her, drawing the hood up over her thick brown hair. She stared at him, still dazed with loss, her eyes expressionless: and it seemed now that the squire was many years her senior. She obeyed him without question.

'We will ride side by side when the track is wide enough; otherwise, I shall lead you, my lady. The pack-mare will follow your mount, for she is his mother.'

'A better one than I, who leaves my son to strangers.'

Bartholomew looked at her sharply, then reached out his hand with the gesture that had been Duke's and touched her glove. Had he not done so, she would have returned to Kirkburn.

They kept to the high moors and unfrequented tracks, adding many miles to the journey. On the first night they did not stop for sleep or food, but, at midday, rested the horses in a cave and cooked a meal; then they pressed on again. The weather was still sharp and dry. They could see great distances over the desolate moor. They glanced behind frequently.

The sun sank red as fire in a blazing sky while hills and low cloud turned from grey to bluish-purple. Looking back,

Lucia saw a movement along the sharp line where hill and sky met.

'They have found us,' she said tonelessly.

Bartholomew's eyes narrowed under his lifted palm.

'Not yet,' he replied, looking around him quickly, wishing for the cave where they had rested at midday. The wide moor offered no protection for two people and three horses. He studied the sky in the north-easterly direction; it was grey and thick with cloud. It would not silhouette their figures as the fiery sunset was doing to their pursuers'. He decided to hide by merging with landscape.

'My lady, fasten your coat tightly and let the hood shade your face. Do not remove your gloves. And, I pray you, keep your foot and that length of white lace hidden. Now, sit your horse without moving.'

He held the reins of his own mount and of the pack-mare, standing between them, quieting them with his voice.

The riders approached out of the sunset. One of their horses whinnied sharply and Lucia sat tense, fearful in case her own mount should answer.

Bartholomew knew that if the riders did not change course within a few minutes, they would be upon them. He prayed, his bright head bowed. And Lucia looked down at him and loved him for his courage. She was never to forget the sight of him standing there between the horses, defence-less and upright and very young. Duke had looked like that…

With much shouting and whip-waving, the riders passed within a quarter of a mile of the spot where the others waited. Darkness fell.

Lucia and Bartholomew moved forward again cautiously, but the horses were stumbling now with weari-ness. A thorn-tree clawed viciously at Lucia's skirt out of the darkness, and when the squire stopped to disentangle it, he tripped over a pile of stones. These he examined with growing interest.

'A shepherd's shelter,' he said triumphantly, 'built for summer pasturing of sheep up here.'

He cleared the entrance and crawled inside. There was room to stand up. There was a hole in the earth roof for the passage of smoke. The sunken floor was dry.

He brought Lucia inside and lit a fire, then tended the horses while she prepared a meal.

Afterwards, they huddled in their clothes, their bones aching, their hands stretched out to the fire.

'The animals need several hours' rest,' he said.

'Yes.' She was thinking how impossible this journey would have been without his leadership. 'Bartholomew – sit by me.' He was strength and warmth to her. She leaned against him and drew his arm about her shoulders. In the glow of the firelight, his profile and the colour of his hair were like Duke's.

'Kiss me,' she said.

His mouth was very gentle, his hand as timid as a young animal. She took his hand in both of hers and pressed it against her throat as though it were the child she had left behind. The youth sighed and kissed her again, long and hard on the mouth.

She unbraided her hair and lay down, holding out the leather coat from her side.

'Lie close to me. It is cold and the horses must rest.'

Suddenly, he put his head on her arm and began to sob like a child.

'I know how it is,' she said gently, stroking his hair. 'Tomorrow or the day after, we will part, perhaps forever. You believe you will miss me, that such an hour as this will never come again. But there are many women in the world, Bartholomew, when you are ready for them.'

'No one,' he whispered. 'No one ever but you.'

'I am another man's wife, returning to a lover. Forget me.'

'I will never forget you. I will think of you all my life and seek you again and again.'

The journey which should have taken two days was still not ended on the morning of the third. In their anxiety to avoid contact with the regular routes, the travellers had strayed far. The horses were exhausted and all food at an end. Now dense fog lay over the entire countryside, icy and penetrating.

Lucia was breathing with great difficult, owing to a pain across her chest. She rode leaning forward, pretending to stare into the fog but knowing that the red mist before her eyes was a recurrence of the fever she had suffered at Castleton.

The youth, too, was exhausted beyond speech. He had walked many miles since dawn, leading the bewildered horses, and his feet were now bare of all covering.

At midday, a red disc of sun showed briefly, followed by gloom and then darkness. Lucia was unconscious now of anything except the pain within her. She knew that they were riding through wooded country only because she tasted blood from cuts on her face.

Bartholomew halted the horses and held up his arms to her.

'Lucia, you are home! *Home...*'

She did not understand his words.

He led her to the gates of Kilton, barred for the early darkness. She lay forward, face downwards, over the horse's neck, not recognising the castle.

'Goodbye, my lady,' Bartholomew said.

He raised his hand, holding a stone to throw at the gate.

'You – you are going away?' she asked despairingly.

'No one must know that you have been alone with me. Do not speak of me. I will travel on…'

She nodded dully. He flung the stone at the gate and a dog began to bark inside.

'Goodbye, Lucia,' he said before turning away quickly. The fog swallowed him at once. The pack-mare stood for a moment, irresolute, before she, too, dragged herself into the thick darkness of the wood, following Bartholomew as she had done these many miles.

A lantern flashed from the look-out window and a voice said wonderingly:

'A lady!'

The gates began to open slowly and the lights of Kilton showed blurred and reddish through the fog. Lucia felt herself being led inside, every movement a separate agony. In one instant of clarity, she saw the face of the red-headed, squint-eyed boy who used to wait for her in the early mornings. She heard running footsteps and her name being shouted before she fell down into a sea of upraised arms.

Now it seemed to her that she was in the carved bed under the popinjays. Her aunt and uncle and all her cousins were grouped around. Friar Alan was there at her feet, praying as though over the dead, and Duke was by her side, his hand on hers. But this was the self-same dream she had dreamed in the fortress of Castleton before the child was born. Soon she would awake to the pain of green apples; she would writhe and scream; a serpent would tighten itself around her waist, pressing the bones inwards, splintering them until even the flesh tore.

She relived the birth of Duke's son while sweat ran

down her face. And afterwards she talked and wept and talked again – of the rats, of the sickly child, of her father-in-law's cruelty and her husband's infidelity; of her loneliness and shame; of her ride over the moors, trying to reach Kilton... And, as though caution worked even in her fevered brain, she insisted that she had made the journey alone, or that her cousin, Duke, had accompanied her. Of this later, she became convinced, describing in detail his face, his hair in the firelight, his hand over hers on the rein.

Now the group around the bed exchanged uneasy glances with one another. Isabel was sobbing, the girls terror-stricken. Marmaduke and the priest wrestling with doubts which had never been fully allayed since the wedding.

But Duke, looking ten years older since the day Lucia had ridden out of Kilton with her husband, stood up suddenly and stared from the praying friar to his silent parents and back again.

'She is my wife,' he said. There was no defiance in his tone, only a weary reasonableness. 'I have watched her bear my son. If she lives, no one shall ever send her away from Kilton again.'

They did not argue with him, then or afterwards. Duke was the eldest son, and heir to Kilton; he was no longer a boy. The forced marriage, to which all the adults here had been a party, weighed heavy on their consciences, and they wished that they had let Duke have his way in the first place, either by battle or by direct plea to the King.

Maybe better now than not at all.

They took turns to rest and watch, but Duke ignored them, never leaving Lucia's side himself. Sometimes she knew that he was there, and her hand caressed him. On the fifth night, when his mother came to take over the vigil, he sent her away.

'Lucia is better,' Duke said. 'She sleeps naturally. So shall I, now.'

He turned back the coverings of the popinjay bed and lay beside her, his arm under her head. When his father came in the morning they were still sleeping, and the older man stood and watched them for a moment before, sighing, he turned away.

6

I t was a day of thin February sunshine in the year 1296. Lucia and her aunt Isabel were busily sorting out the summer linen. It came in white layers out of herb-scented wooden boxes – sheets and altar cloths, shirts and kirtles – and was stacked steadily higher around the kneeling women like piling snow.

'My back aches,' Isabel said, rising with difficulty. She went over to the window near her bed and looked out. 'Who is that stranger with your uncle, Lucia?'

'Let me see!'

The two women leaned far out. Marmaduke was coming from the stables where the red-headed lad was tending a strange horse. The horse's owner was walking towards the outer stair with Marmaduke. The women heard them cross the Great Hall and then the long corridor to the private apartments.

Isabel opened the door and Marmaduke bellowed:

'Ah, there you are, my love! We have a visitor – from the King.'

The King's messenger looked cold and hungry, but declined Isabel's offer of hospitality.

'It is better that I reach Mulgrave before nightfall,' he explained. 'Time is short.' He swallowed some wine, bowed and was gone.

Marmaduke sank down among the piles of linen on the bed.

'Trouble again in Scotland,' he said. 'Never a day's quiet there since Alexander died. Now Cressingham and de Warenne have stirred all the factions up at once and the King is hell-bent to help them.'

Marmaduke poked gloomily at a white lace bedspread with his stable-fouled toe. Isabel scooped the spread to safety and pretended to be very occupied, but she watched her husband covertly, and Lucia watched them both quite openly, sprawling on the floor with her chin in her hands.

'Well?' Isabel mumbled, holding a sheet with her chin pressed against her throat.

'Hoh? Oh – ah – we shall have to go, I suppose.'

'To Scotland?'

'To Newcastle at the outset. Edward has summoned his troops there for the first day of March.'

'I see,' Isabel said, her back to him.

Lucia considered the matter for a while.

'Are you taking Duke, Uncle?'

'Er – oh, yes. Yes. He's fully fledged now, have to go. Robert can squire for him. I'll have William. Where *is* Duke? There's six months' work to do in three weeks…'

Marmaduke heaved himself off the bed, making new chaos of the linen, and went off grumbling about spring sowings and sheep shearing. He did not look at Isabel but, as he went by, he touched her arm lingeringly. A single stab of jealousy transfixed Lucia that here was a love greater, an understanding deeper, a friendship more massive than she and Duke could hope to achieve, ever, in their unblessed alliance. And she longed for marriage to Duke, and children by him. He was kind and gentle like his father and mother. Given time, he would be wise and mature. Given time...

THE MONTH of February galloped to a close in a frenzy of preparation at Kilton. Already it was the day of departure. The weather was brilliant. The wind shouted and buffeted. The earth, hard as steel, magnified every sound until all was confusion.

In every open space around the castle, men and horses jostled. Polished armour glinted. Pages wiped their noses on their sleeves and the wind whipped the standards. Women tried to press little parcels of food on embarrassed young men who repeated that they didn't need anything else, Mother, honestly, and one solemn child, red-eared, blue-faced with cold, was engrossed in plaiting two horses' tails together.

Uncle Marmaduke was already mounted. Huge and resplendent in plum-coloured velvet with cloak-lining in the de Thweng blue and silver, he moved towards the gates and all the others fell into line beside or behind him. Duke, in full knightly regalia, was on his father's right, his brand-new armour bright as silver, his tunic unstained by rust, his small fair hands and face mottled a curious purple where cold and excitement mingled in his blood. Younger brothers William and Robert paged behind. Little Thomas, Nicholas and John ran alongside, too young to have any part in this procession once it passed the gates.

Isabel wept into her husband's sleeve, keeping pace with his horse until the narrow gateway pushed her aside.

Then she sat down plumply on the mounting-stone and cried and cried, while the unheeding throng swept by. Her daughters Margaret, Lucia and Catherine were far too busy waving and shouting from the top of the West Ditch to comfort their mother.

But the other Lucia stood apart. Her farewells had been made under the green popinjays, and now she let her lover go from her without further word or touch. It was his adventure, her tragedy. She observed the cavalcade but was no part of it until, right at the end, the sight of a laughing boy's face flashed into her vision and her heart stood still: a de Thweng face, fine-skinned, the teeth and eyeballs flashing white, the enormous charm now fully directed on a tearful young girl.

Fascinated, Lucia watched their unabashed embrace, their lips moist from kissing.

'Come back soon, love,' the girl called, her arms still outstretched from the caress.

The boy turned, laughing and waving.

He was Lucia's half-brother, illegitimate son of her father. A little part of her, never before considered, went out of Kilton with him that day; an unreturning part.

THE SUMMERS of '96 and '97 went by and the North was a land of women and growing children and old men. Every boy had been thrown into the Scottish campaign by a King whose energies had once made the laws of England but were now directed into a single stream of desire for the suppression of the Scots.

When the eleventh of September dawned, the residents of Kilton were not to know that it would differ from any other day. They had heard that William Wallace was in a strong position on the north side of the River Forth, not far from Stirling Castle. The King's army was closing in. That was all they knew or heard until two days later.

It was a hot, still afternoon. The smell of ripening fruit was heavy in the bee-loud air, the sky fogged with heat all around the horizon.

Lucia said to her aunt:

'I shall go and see if the blackberries are ripe enough to pick yet around the Ditch. Will you come?'

Isabel fanned her shining face.

'No, dear. It's too hot. I don't know what drives you, Lucia!'

But Lucia knew. There was a fierce fund of energy within her which only Duke could unleash to creative purpose. She had a feeling of waste and of futility which Isabel, fulfilled, could never understand.

She took two flat baskets from the kitchens and went out, tying a white linen scarf around her hair so that the sun would not make it brittle. The lavender satin of her dress felt cool against her bare legs as she walked, but she envied her three young boy cousins when she passed them, splashing about almost naked in the horse-trough.

'Coming to gather blackberries with me?' she called.

'No,' they shouted ungraciously and in unison.

Lonely, she walked on. There was a very old man sitting outside the gate and she gave him a honeycake for alms.

'Soldier – up the road,' the old man mumbled, dribbling on his beard.

'A *soldier*, here?'

He nodded, trying to bite the cake with toothless gums.

'Dying,' he added, without compassion.

'Which way?'

A crooked finger pointed waveringly. Lucia began to walk fast, faster, along the white road.

The soldier lay in a little dark heap, face downward. He was bleeding from the mouth and the blood was bright and frothy on the sun-baked dust. She half-turned him on to his side.

'Where were you going when you fell?'

'Anywhere – away from Stirling Bridge.'

His words were thick with blood.

'In whose company were you fighting?'

'De Thweng.'

She wiped his mouth with the scarf from her head. Blood was choking him and he might not be able to speak again. His horse limped out of the bushes and stood over him, head drooping.

'Are all the de Thwengs safe?'

After a long time he shook his head once.

She bent close so that her forehead touched his. She could smell his blood and his sweat and his approaching death.

'Who is dead? Sir Marmaduke, the baron?'

Again an agonising pause, then a shake of the head.

'The younger sons, squires William and Robert?'

'No.'

She drew a breath of furnace air.

'Marmaduke – the younger?'

The soldier was beyond speech or movement She heaved him upright and he moaned. She saw the long wound in his side. She shook him without pity.

'Marmaduke!' she screamed. 'The heir. Is he safe? *Tell me!*'

The soldier opened his eyes, but they were blind.

'Dead,' he whispered, and bowed his head. His last breath stopping in his throat.

She left him lying in the roadway and walked slowly towards Kilton, her hands empty. The soldier's horse followed her with trailing rein.

Now THE DAYS and the nights followed each other in unending darkness, for Lucia kept the bed-curtains drawn tightly against the sun and only arose to wander about the sleeping house when there was no moonlight. She slept only for nightmares and always awoke with terrible suddenness to the same instant reality: Duke was dead.

Now she must know the manner of his death, every detail of it. This idea obsessed her. There had been much commotion inside the castle for several days – the gates being opened after sundown to admit fugitives from Scotland, soldiers tramping about in the Hall. Many of these men must know what happened. Isabel must know.

Isabel... what of her? Duke was her son. Her loss was as great as Lucia's.

Ashamed, she got up and dressed. It was late at night, but she went to her aunt's apartment.

Isabel was still fully clothed and tapers burned flickeringly in the draught from the loosely shuttered windows. She was composed, her voice quiet.

'Lucia, it is kind of you to come to me, dear.'

'Kind to have left you without help or comfort for – how long, Aunt?' her lip quivered.

'Too long to live in the dark. Come and sit by me. I have been too busy for grief and will not admit it now.'

Lucia, at first blinded by the taper light, now saw with shock that a man was lying on her aunt's bed.

'The place is full of wounded,' Isabel said. 'Your uncle ordered as many as possible to be cared for here, for he wanted only sound men with him in Stirling Castle.'

'My uncle is inside Stirling?'

'He is in command,' Isabel said tonelessly. 'De Warenne entrusted it to him; a doubtful honour. It is provisioned for six weeks.'

'And then?'

'His orders are to hold out for ten weeks against the besieging Wallace. Then he is to be relieved.'

'Four weeks – without food…' Lucia wished she had not said that.

'Yes.' Isabel folded her hands. And Lucia remembered the love that was between her aunt and uncle and wondered if, after all, the quick death of the beloved were not preferable to the slow uncertain torture.

The man on the bed groaned and Isabel arose to attend to him. Her movements were stiff and slow with weariness.

'Aunt Isabel, go to my bed. Let me stay here with this man.'

'You feel well enough?'

'If you do, so must I.'

Gratefully, Isabel dragged her feet to he door and along the corridor, sighing at every step.

One by one, the tapers burned out, dying in spirals of grey smoke. The September night was chilly, and Lucia hastened to cover the wounded man more closely against the cold.

'Are you not cold also, lady?' he asked out of the darkness.

'No, I feel nothing.'

'I feel the throbbing of my wounds,' he said, 'and the bitterness of regret for dead men.'

'Do you want to tell me about the battle?'

'There was nothing to make it differ from other battles, lady. Dust blotting out the sun. The noise of clashing weapons like a forge in Hell. Friend killing friend in sudden panic when gloom and dust and noise made friend and foe alike. That's any battle, lady, after the first orderly charge.'

'But at Stirling Bridge?'

'At Stirling Bridge there was a river. And, in the distance, a castle. After a while, we saw a blazing bridge and the splash of bodies falling into the water. That's all I'll remember to set it apart.'

'Were you close by the de Thwengs during the fighting?'

'If I were not, I would be dead now.'

'Yet one of the de Thwengs died...'

'Two. The heir and Robert's bastard. They died together.'

'You saw it happen?'

'I saw them spitted on one spear.'

She tried to speak and could not.

'Neither one was in front,' the voice continued. 'They were fighting back to back. They were so alike that they drew my notice, just for the instant. The horses were gone off, wild. I saw the gleam of the six-foot spear, and it must have found both hearts, for they were of equal height. For a long moment, they stood together, dead, but supporting each other—'

'—Then?'

'Then I had other things to do, lady. There were ten Scots to every man of us.'

She was silent.

'Have I made you feel sick, lady? I am sorry. I am a rough soldier.'

'No. I thank you.'

She went over to the window and looked through a

crack in the shutter. Dawn was grey in a tattered sky. She felt nothing, neither cold nor sick.

Behind her, the man on the bed began to snore.

THIRTEEN WEEKS DRAGGED BY, and the Feast of Christmas came joylessly to Kilton with the news that Marmaduke had surrendered Stirling to Wallace. Unrelieved by the promised help, and starving, Marmaduke drew up his conditions: that he and his men be allowed to retire unmolested, with their arms, to the nearest fortress. Wallace agreed, then treacherously set upon the men and imprisoned their commander at Dunbarton.

7

The Friar's room in the apsidal tower had a deserted appearance these days. Alan himself still spent most of his time there, but his morning classes were now for little Nicholas only, the youngest of the de Thweng children. The three girls were married, two of the older boys had gone away to study in church seminaries, and William – the heir after Duke's death – much occupied in his courtship of the titian-haired Catherine de Furnival.

Lucia visited the ageing Friar most afternoons. The room held bitter-sweet memories for her of bright-haired children jostling on its cramped benches, and in the Friar's company she recovered a little of her own youthful animation, if only in argument, for she and Alan had seldom agreed on any point.

Today, she made patterns in the dust of the window-ledge with her finger and only half-listened to his droning.

'… Time,' he was saying, 'heals most wounds, my child. Your life is not ended. At least two-thirds of it stretches out before you. I beg of you, Lucia, to begin again – to live rather than to exist.'

Impatiently, she swept the dust on to the hem of his rough gown. He made no move to shake it off but contemplated it resignedly.

'You think I have forgotten Duke?' she demanded.

'No, of course not, daughter—'

'—But it is nearly four years since you read the burial service for him in St. Peter's while his body lay rotting in Scotland. You consider that I have had ample time to recover, is that it?'

He sighed.

'Time is not measured in years for the heart.'

She regarded him coolly.

'I wonder how you know that?'

He laughed thinly.

'Aged old stick that I am!'

Friendship crept into her eyes.

'At first,' she said softly, 'I was numbed and unbelieving. Agony followed – anticipated agony. I remember once, in the Hall, as a child, Duke was swinging me around, his hands clasped about my chest, and I caught my ankle on a table leg sharply and with great force. But I felt no pain as Duke unclasped me. I bent down and touched the bone. Still, there was no pain, no feeling. Yet I remember thinking very clearly, "In a moment, the pain will come," and I became weak and faint at the idea, not the actuality. I suffered twice. It was the same with Duke's death – fear of pain first, then the actual pain.

'I withdrew myself into dreams and memories and fantasies. Now, no morning dawns that I do not reach out my hand to his created image beside me.'

The Friar rolled up a manuscript and pushed it back on a high shelf with hundreds of others. Dust showered down. He remained standing.

'Why not touch reality instead? Duke's flesh is still living and growing.'

'My son was taken away from me,' she said quietly, 'and given to the woman who shared my husband's bed.'

'You can reclaim your son and forgive your husband.'

The Friar was standing close to her, looking down upon her. Gently, his old hand brushed some dust from her hair.

'Lucia, return to William le Latimer.'

'No.'

'Lucia, return to Duke's son.'

'I cannot.'

'You must.'

She sprang up to face him.

'Your advice was always that of a ghost, a corpse, a crab, a dead twig in the forest, Alan. How can you order anyone how to live? Have you ever lived?'

'Yes,' he said quietly. 'I have seen every city in Europe and many in the East. I have eaten with their people.'

'Tush,' Lucia said, bundling the long end of her cloak under one arm, the signal for departure. Alan shrugged. He was accustomed to her outbursts and believed that they did her good. They affected him no more than water affects a duck, so long as her language remained reasonable, which was not always the case.

'You are an embarrassment to the family here, Lucia.'

'*What?*' She had reached the door.

'Do not misunderstand me,' he continued, unperturbed. 'They love you as their own. But your Uncle Marmaduke has become a powerful figure in the land. Honours have been heaped upon him by the King for his service in Scotland. When he retires – which must be soon, Lucia: he is no longer young – should it not be to peace at last, instead of to unending strife with the le Latimers?'

The long end of the cloak fell to the floor. Nobody had

spoken so plainly to Lucia since Duke's death, and she was shocked. The Friar knew that she needed time now to think. He went out quietly.

Lucia sat down on the school bench and tried to consider Alan's words. It was true indeed that Marmaduke had gained great distinction after his release from Dunbarton. He was now a famous soldier. Every time he visited Kilton from the wars, he brought some new honour with him.

Ah, these visits from Scotland! They were times of frenzied rejoicing in the castle. No weighty family matters were ever discussed – except the girls' dowries! – and Marmaduke had kept any trouble with the le Latimers to himself. How much trouble had there been? And was Lucia's continued presence here likely to affect the happiness of young William, the heir, when he married Catherine de Furnival, as well as the happiness and security of her aunt and uncle?

'Blind and foolish for four years,' she whispered. 'Are they never to have peace from you? It seems that they have reared a large family with less trouble than they have reared you alone.'

That night, in St. Peter's chapel, she came to her decision to return to William le Latimer at Kirkburn. The decision was prompted mainly by her love for Marmaduke and Isabel, but also by her loneliness for Duke's child and by the very aimlessness of her own life, so far removed from the energetic and creative nature of de Thweng.

'Perhaps,' she prayed hopefully, 'I shall die soon…'

She had often prayed thus in four years. Now in her early twenties, she had not the slightest hope that there could be any happiness left for her in life.

When she told her aunt and uncle of what she was about to do, she gave them no hint of its mainspring.

'My place is with my son,' she explained desperately. 'He has lived too long without me and I without him.'

They questioned her closely, but she did not depart from that explanation, and in the end they believed her.

Now messages were exchanged between Kilton and Kirkburn and, as a result, a meeting was arranged of Marmaduke de Thweng with William le Latimer the elder, in the brand new palace-fortress of Danby, not yet quite completed.

The two had not met for many years – years filled for both with soldiering and exile – and they studied each other carefully as they walked from courtyard to castle.

'The Scottish scenery does you good, de Thweng,' le Latimer said in his light, dry voice, noting that Marmaduke was broader and ruddier than ever. But Marmaduke, looking down upon the smaller man, knew that he could not truthfully compliment him upon his appearance: wounds from the Gascony campaign had written a forewarning of death upon the wrinkled face.

They stood and looked upward at the splendid building of new Danby Castle, its creamy stones as yet unweathered to the greyish green of Cleveland.

'You are a good architect, le Latimer. If the materials have been as luckily come by as the land, may you prosper here!' Marmaduke could not restrain himself from the sly dig, for it galled him to remember that this was de Brus land.

Le Latimer stiffened defensively.

'The King confirmed my ownership of all when your niece deserted my son.'

De Thweng laughed outright, his envy gone in the face of the other's discomfort.

'Will the King then again pervert the royal prerogative and drive you out when my niece returns to your son? But

come, let us discuss this matter now. I have no wish to ride
through Danby in the dark, for only you may hunt there by
the grace of his outraged Majesty – and you might put a
spear in my ribs in error for a boar…'

The oblique barbs unsettled le Latimer, but he was
determined to display his ill-gotten property to its fullest
advantage. The design of the castle was almost a hundred
years ahead of its time, for the North of England, in grace
and comfort. The quadrangular building had towers at the
angles of the small courtyard and the views were breath-
taking, of moor and forest and rich pastureland. Le
Latimer lingered over each feature for the benefit of his
guest but, curiously, only permitted him a quick glance at
the outer walls. Then they went indoors for meat and wine.

'Well,' the Lord of Danby enquired, 'you still consider
me a good builder?'

Marmaduke drank mightily.

'Too good to employ such a poor stonemason.'

'What do you mean?' the other choked.

'He who carved the shields on the outer wall: de Brus,
de Roos, le Latimer – but no de Thweng!'

Now le Latimer blustered.

'Why should I include her arms? She has disgraced us
all.'

'She has also brought you most of what you own. This
tankard here from which I drink used to grace Kilton's
High Table. Likewise that salt-cellar there. The tapestry on
your east wall is from St. Peter's. See? Handle all with
caution, le Latimer. The King is old and forgetful. Only by
Lucia's return to your son at Kirkburn is your title strong.
If she stays, all is well.'

'You said a moment ago that her return might jeopar-
dise my property. Which do you mean?'

'Both.'

Le Latimer shook with rage while Marmaduke, unconcernedly, went on eating his meat.

'If she deserts him again,' le Latimer said through clenched teeth, 'I will make a further claim against her.'

'Greed is dangerous, my friend. You might lose all. It is in your interests, le Latimer, and in the interests of your son and his heirs, to make certain that Lucia stays this time. If I were in your position – which heaven forbid! – I would remove certain annoyances from Lucia's path.'

'Such as—?'

'Such as William's mistress, Mary Godwin from Castleton.'

'Oh, that. Very well. He would never have taken her in the first place had I been at home to supervise the household.'

'That is another thing: your supervision, as you term it. Your interference. It must cease. My niece has never been able to abide you. You will keep out of her way.'

'I—'

'You are fully occupied here. That is correct. See that it remains so.'

There was a sullen silence; then le Latimer said:

'It wants only an hour to darkness, de Thweng.'

Marmaduke's mouth twitched in a smile at the manner of his dismissal, but he was well enough pleased with the visit to make no further comment, and he was happier for Lucia's sake than previously.

'Goodbye, le Latimer. Long may you enjoy your property. It grieves me to see you so insecure and ill at ease.'

'Damn you, de Thweng. Goodbye.'

During the following month, Lucia returned to Kirk-burn. The manor house had been smartened considerably for her arrival, and retainers lined the courtyard to bid her welcome. Her husband and seven-year-old son awaited her within.

As soon as she entered the house, the old malevolence pressed upon her from every wall. Then she saw her son's face, closed and resentful, and she drew a deep breath to give her strength. She kissed him and he turned his head away, not in shyness but in malice.

'Give him time,' William mumbled. 'The child is bewildered.'

That night, husband and wife slept in the same bed, and William, under Mary Godwin's tuition, appeared to have learned some of the rudiments of love-making. Lucia responded to him. It was many years since a man had caressed her.

Very shortly, however, the screams of their son from the adjoining room sent them both hurrying to his side. He was in a high fever. The only word which he spoke was:

'Mary!'

This continued for two days and the child was losing strength. William, demented, dragged Lucia outside the door and demanded that Mary Godwin be sent for without delay.

Their marriage lay in the balance, weighed by the child's life.

'Let the nurse be sent for,' Lucia ordered.

She knew she had lost the brief battle.

Now the claims of Scotland again intervened. William was summoned to muster a force and proceed northward without delay. Two women bade him farewell. Only one was to welcome his return.

With William gone and the child back in Mary's care, Lucia began to wander further and further from Kirkburn for longer and longer periods in search of pleasures to fill her empty life. She became well-known in castle and manor house as a guest whose reckless gaiety kept gatherings fully awake all night. Next day, she would ride with the hunt, her eyes undimmed, her cheeks glowing. Few people could keep pace with her, but she had a retinue of admirers from which she picked and chose, replacing weary with fresh from one sunrise to another.

The legend of 'the Helen of Cleveland' grew apace, but was yet nowhere near its peak.

Kilton Castle those days was a place where gaiety and young company abounded. William de Thweng, the heir, had married his red-headed Catherine, and they gathered around them friends and relatives from all over Cleveland for hunts and banquets. Lucia was a frequent visitor, usually staying a week or more when she came, and there sprang up a warm friendship between herself and Catherine.

'Lucia,' Catherine said one evening, sitting on the edge of the popinjay bed, 'guess who's home from the wars and coming tonight?'

'Tell me,' Lucia smiled, patting milk on her face.

'Peter de Mauley from Mulgrave.'

'Oh!'

'Are you not glad?'

'I – I don't know. He was a child when I last saw him. What kind of young man is he now?'

'Very handsome. Very clever.'

'Ummm.'

'Well, get dressed, Lucia. Everyone comes to see *you*, you know, when you're here. Oh, I wish I were like you…'

Lucia looked in astonishment at her cousin's wife; at the moon-white skin, the little teeth, the blue-grey eyes, the glory of red-gold hair.

'Why on earth should you wish to be like me, Catherine?'

'Because you draw people to you like cold hands to a fire. Because you are never tired or frightened or confused. Because whatever dress you wear you transform into a royal gown. And because your eyes, behind the tapers, have golden flecks in them while you talk with more wit than a man. There!'

They laughed and embraced.

'Catherine, you are a very beautiful woman, happily married, mistress of a lovely estate. Do not envy such as I am.'

Together, they went down to the other apartment where Catherine's dresses were stored, and chose what she should wear that night.

Lucia had no difficulty in recognising Peter de Mauley. The dark hair and sallow skin; the high, rounded line of the cheek, contrasting with pointed chin; the narrow, upward-slanting eyes – these were the features she had noted years previously when he rode out of the woods towards her and Duke. His coming, then, had brought misfortune in its wake. Now it was she who approached him.

'Peter, how pleasant to meet you at Kilton again after so many years!'

He bowed deeply, his eyes never leaving her face, but, as he straightened again, the gaze dropped slowly, appraisingly, to bosom and waist and thigh. She remembered how that look had once outraged her. Now, it excited.

He put out his hand and drew her aside from the throng entering the Hall.

'You are the most beautiful woman in England,' he said. 'May I sit by you?'

She cast her eye quickly over the company assembling at the High Table.

'If you wish.' There were other men, older and more worthy, who should have had Peter's place beside her, but they would be tolerant, knowing that he had been a friend of Duke's.

'That day in the woods,' he said, leaning over to cut her meat for her so that she smelled the herbs he carried in his clothes, 'you wore a green dress. At the banquet that night – I glimpsed you before you ran away! – you were dressed in ivory.'

It was difficult not to be impressed by such a feat of memory, and more difficult not to be complimented by it. Peter was a very handsome man for whom many a maiden in the Hall was already sighing, leaving her meal untouched. But he had eyes for no one except Lucia. True, she had grown accustomed to admiration and flattery of late, and had learned how to invite both, but this was the first time she had drawn gratification from the exercise.

'Tell me about your service in Scotland,' she commanded.

He made a gesture of impatience.

'War is barbaric. There are no words in a civilised tongue to describe it.'

'You dislike fighting?' She was mildly hostile.

'I dislike the idea of mutilation. The human body is perfect.'

'We are told to disregard our bodies.'

'By whom? The Church?'

She smiled.

'I had forgotten you were a pagan, de Mauley.'

She saw the long, white teeth and the dark point of
hair in the centre of the forehead. She saw the fine hand
on the table linen. She looked straight into the cold, green
eyes, knowing that they were noting the golden flecks in
hers in the taper lights. And she knew that she would take
Peter de Mauley as her lover. She was twenty-five, he
twenty-two.

The meal finished with much wine while the minstrels
played. It was a warm evening. People wandered outside.
She had a sudden desire to go down to the river.

Midges skimmed the water's surface and a fish snapped
at them. The big tree on the bank blotted out the lighted
castle. She smelled the herb-sachets in Peter's clothing as
he kissed her.

I like civilised men, she thought, *as much as I dislike uncouth
ones.*

'Come to Mulgrave with me, Lucia,' Peter was saying
now. 'I do as I please there and so could you. Leave the
wretched manor house at Kirkburn—'

'How can I? My husband may return from Scotland at
any time now.'

'Your husband? Bah! Everyone knows the truth of that.
Has he ever taken you?'

'Yes.'

'He would be a cripple if he had not.'

'I must return to Kirkburn tomorrow.'

'The moon is only rising on tonight.'

'No.'

'Very well, if you will not leave Kirkburn of your own
accord, I must send an army to take you away!'

He disengaged himself from her embrace with finality
and made as if to walk off alone. Suddenly she was fright-

ened of being left in this place of memories without human company.

'Peter…'

'Yes?'

'You have heard of my doings these last months?'

He looked at her over his shoulder.

'Could there be anyone in Cleveland who has not?'

'Therefore you think a man has only to beckon and I come?'

He returned to stand beside her in the twilight.

'I have met no man who can claim to be your lover. They say you are still faithful to le Latimer, in the body if not in the spirit. You tease and torment but do not submit. I, alone, know the reason.'

'Why?'

'Because you still have roots, like a tree. While you lived here at Kilton, after Duke's death, you took no other lover for fear of hurting his parents, your guardians. They cared about you, too. If you missed a meal or a night's sleep, they noted it.

'Then, you went to Kirkburn, prepared to be a good wife again and mother to your son. But your husband's woman returned, did she not? Then your husband went away. Suddenly, you were alone – no husband, no child. There was no one to hurt, no one to care whether you came or went.

'For months now, Lucia, you have been practising for the final tilt – testing the strength of your charm on any man who passed but without engaging him in serious combat. Tonight, you are ready. When you leave Kirkburn, you sever the last link with the life you have tried to lead, against every instinct.'

He walked away into the darkening wood, whistling.

≈

KIRKBURN HAD HAD its share of sieges, and regarded without surprise the arrival of a body of armed men from Mulgrave Castle. Their orders were to bring Lucia le Latimer with all her personal belongings, to Lord Peter de Mauley, and those orders were easy to carry out, since there were no men left at Kirkburn fit to resist the invaders; the young and strong were all away in Scotland. Therefore, Lucia went away with the band from Mulgrave quite philosophically, into the June evening, without a backward glance at the graveyard of her marriage. And, watching her departure from an upper window, was Mary Godwin, a slow smile upon her lips. The child played on the floor nearby.

'William, my pet, your lady mother is going away again.'

The child looked briefly towards the window, then went on with his game. His mother had gone away too often of late for it to be of any consequence.

'William,' Mary said, turning her face to him, 'this time she will not be coming back.'

It was not the information she conveyed which caused the child to stare, slack-mouthed. It was the look on Mary Godwin's face: her eyes a blaze of triumph, her thick lips parted in exultation.

8

Mulgrave Castle, near Whitby, was a large and busy place, a walled village set in acres of deep, well-watered woodland. The smell of the North Sea sharpened the air there, but the castle was sheltered by the huge trees which formed a two-mile wall between it and the cliffs.

Joyful company abounded at Mulgrave for the hunts and banquets which Peter de Mauley organised continuously. He was a young baron who had enjoyed complete freedom and enormous wealth from childhood. Now, at twenty-two, he had run through the entire range of normal pleasures and already his conduct was sign-posting a future nickname – *le malolacu,* acquired in later years for the seduction of a nun. It was Peter's vanity to want, always, that which he could not, or should not, have. Therefore the expectancy of Lucia's arrival filled him with a double pleasure: she was to be the first resident mistress he had ever had, and she was another man's wife. Added to these was the lesser pleasure that her presence would greatly enhance his standing with his friends, all of whom were by now acquainted with the growing legend concerning her.

To this end, Peter assembled a glittering company for Lucia's reception to Mulgrave.

She arrived on the evening of the second day, surrounded by twenty armed men and followed by laden pack-horses. The entrance of Balkis into Solomon's court could hardly have been more impressive except that the Lady de Thweng was in a foul temper.

Still sitting her horse, she surveyed the company that had tumbled out from the evening meal into the courtyard. Her tigress eyes singled out the young baron.

'Could you not have come a day's journey to meet me?' she demanded ringingly. Heat, fatigue and the rough company of the men had galled her all the way from Kirkburn, and she was now incensed to find this throng of strangers awaiting her, before she could even change her attire.

Peter flushed and his mouth set sullenly, but even as he walked towards his furious visitor, he had decided how to handle the situation.

He approached very close to her indeed – a lover's advance, his mouth brushing her ear as she dismounted.

'You are tired, beautiful,' he whispered. 'A cool bed, good food and wine awaits you. Come with me. Ignore the others.'

His choice of words was good. After only a little hesitation, she walked with him towards the castle entrance, her hand resting on his arm. A hundred pairs of eyes watched her mercilessly, noting each detail – the dust-dulled hair, the crumpled skirt, the stiff-backed gait of saddle-weariness.

'She is not even *pretty*,' a red-haired girl said loudly as the couple passed. But the girl's companion was staring after Lucia.

'No,' he said absently, 'not pretty at all. Much more than that…'

The red-haired girl's mouth closed like a trap and her plaits swung in a wide arc as she turned to pad away over the cobbles.

Lucia removed her shoes and went to bed in all her clothing, where she slept for twenty hours, unmoving. Peter and his friends were left to kick their heels through the long summer evening and for most of the next day.

While she had slept, the box containing her dresses had been unpacked and the contents pressed free of creases with a hot smoothing iron. They now hung like a rainbow against the wall opposite the bed. She lay considering which one she should wear. Sunlight fingered a vivid red silk with silver scroll embroidery around the neck and wide cuff and hemline. The undersleeves were made of grey and fastened with intricate silver buttons. She had never worn this dress. It had always seemed too vivid, too bold. Now she chose it without hesitation.

As she fastened the heavy silver girdle, Peter approached the apartment for the tenth time that day to know if she were awake. She watched his face as he looked at her, drawing confidence from his flush of pride.

'Welcome to Mulgrave, Lucia,' he said solemnly. 'You were in no mood yesterday for even that civility.'

Laughing, they went downstairs together and out on to the sunny lawn, where four young men were playing a ball game before a large audience. Up on the sun balcony ladies sewed and gossiped, and there was music from a little pavilion near the river. For Lucia's new role, it was a splendid setting.

Her presence at Mulgrave as Peter's mistress caused tremendous excitement, and, within a few weeks, another occurrence enhanced the whole affair. The King sent his

Precept to the Sheriff of Yorkshire 'to make strict search for her and, in case he did find her, raise the power of the County and carry her back to Kirkburn'.

Peter himself read out a copy of this Precept from the High Table and everyone laughed uproariously, and all the men present swore to protect Lucia from the Sheriff. Indeed, quite a game was made of it for several days, and new guests arriving at the castle were asked to prove that they were not, in fact, the Sheriff of Yorkshire!

However, the King's man never came to Mulgrave, although it was well known throughout the countryside that Lucia was there. Gradually the excitement died down, but it would be untrue to say that tranquillity entered into the relationship of Lucia with Peter de Mauley.

The truth was that she had found him a poor lover from the start. His languid fastidiousness, his jealousy, his passion for lengthy discussion, his vanity – these things infuriated her increasingly. Her tantrums and upbraidings became more frequent. Her refusals to allow him near her were now made publicly and with more force.

Two friends of Peter's, discussing a recent quarrel between the lovers, found that Lucia was the cause of all the trouble.

'She is far too old for him,' one said, with a great deal of head-shaking.

'Too mature,' said the other, who envied Peter.

'He is not accustomed to that kind of woman, all pride and imperiousness.'

'True. His past loves have been submissive – dairy-maids and the like. And a few daughters-of-the-vanquished up in Scotland.'

'If he could handle a Scottish wench, he should find Lucia de Thweng an angel.'

'No woman is an angel when she is bored.'

'Why should she be bored? He is cultured and travelled, a great wit, game for anything. He has made her the
mistress of Mulgrave and defied the King and the le
Latimers by keeping her here. She should, at least, be
grateful.'

'A de Thweng grateful? They honour you by their
company. Mark my words, one day she will sweep out of
here – with a new lover, probably – and suddenly the place
will be cold and dark, and we will wonder what it was we
once enjoyed…'

A prophecy indeed. That same night, Lucia heard for
the first time the name of Nicholas de Menyll, and, leaning
forward across the High Table, she followed the conversation with interest. A singularly warlike baron this de Menyll
appeared to be from what was said of him. Men feared
him. Women avoided him. He hunted where he wished,
royal property or no. And he had once taken minor orders
but now had few dealings with the Church.

'He has been seen around here lately, too!' a woman
sitting near Lucia said loudly.

'Who?' Peter demanded with his mouth full.

'Nicholas de Menyll.'

The woman crossed herself quickly and, all at once,
everybody stopped talking.

Peter said deliberately.

'Nonsense. If de Menyll were here, he would have
come to see me.'

Somebody laughed shrilly, then remembered that
indeed a kind of friendship did exist between the houses of
Mulgrave and Whorlton – mainly for the purpose of
getting each other out of trouble – and choked the laugh
midway.

Lucia turned to Peter.

'Who is this de Menyll?'

Peter grimaced.

'The Baron of Whorlton, twenty-nine-year-old murderer and seducer!'

Now everyone laughed at once, but Lucia persisted above the uproar.

'What is his appearance?'

'Excessively tall. Black curling hair. Eyes like a madman. Think you will know him in the dark, my love?'

Unsmilingly, Lucia nodded.

'I think I will know him,' she said.

HER TWO-MONTH RESIDENCE at Mulgrave had done Lucia no service. Life there, necessarily confined because of the threat of being returned to her husband by the Sheriff, had told upon her looks and figure. The sharp angle of jaw and chin had blurred. Her skin, always inclined to be sallow, had yellowed further, and her eyes were tired.

She drove herself to furious exertion and wore out anyone who lived in constant contact with her by her increasing demands for amusement, as opposed to her former ability to amuse others. De Mauley lived in terror of her outbursts, and scoured the countryside to bring home new guests to relieve her boredom with himself. This latter element turned down the corners of her mouth and gave her face an expression of irritation and discontent.

She was ill-pleased with her life. Even minor pleasure, like visits to nearby Whitby, were fraught with fears and imaginings of the Sheriff's hand, although she admitted those fears to no one since the whole affair had been treated as a joke at Mulgrave. It had never been a joke to Lucia, but she maintained an air of bravado.

She wanted freedom. She wanted a protector. Therefore, she seized upon the name and reputation of Nicholas de Menyll and carried it about in her mind, willing a meeting with him, not doubting her ability to make him do as she wished. The de Thwengs had always conquered easily, but by charm, not heavy-handedness. And Lucia was taking less and less trouble to charm. Her tempers became more violent with frequency, and when she was aroused her language would have shamed a common soldier.

Yet she remained a woman above the rest, mature enough to know that her pounding energy was at constant odds with the aimlessness of her life, humble enough to wish for a man of her own kind.

She had no home to go to. The only escape from Mulgrave was with a man as ruthless and as defiant of the law as the Baron de Menyll. A lesser woman than Lucia de Thweng might have chosen to stay where she was. Only recently the Baron had murdered an entire family at Easby: his pardon was a masterpiece of legal evasion, hinging mainly on the fact that, as a youth, he had taken Clerk's Orders and carried a Bishop's cup at a consecration!

～

THE HUNT WENT by Foss Mill, crossed the stream above the dark pool and clattered over the flagstones outside the mill house. It was early morning. Mist still shrouded the August sun.

From the bank by the mill pool, a tall thin man was fishing. He was roughly dressed in green worsted and brown leather. His dog, a huge Irish wolfhound, lay watchfully by his feet, and his horse cropped quietly nearby.

Peter de Mauley stood up in his stirrups and shouted:

'De Menyll! Oi! Nicholas…'

The fisherman looked up lazily, waved and then beckoned. Peter forded the stream again, the others following – some eagerly, most of them dubiously.

Lucia, unaware of the fisherman's identity because she had been out of earshot when Peter called his name, came last without haste.

'Have you caught anything?' Peter shouted, galloping down the bank.

Nicholas stretched himself to his full enormous height.

'You frighten every fish from here to Whitby with your clamour,' he said, flinging his bait into the water. Immediately a large trout leapt after it, and everybody except the fuming baron shook with mirth.

'Good,' Peter said, wiping his eyes. 'Now you must come and break your fast with us.'

Nicholas wound his fishing-line about his waist, stuck some hooks into his tattered green tunic and clicked his fingers at horse and dog.

'I thank you, no,' he said. 'Halls in this weather smell only of rancid butter and bad meat.'

Lucia rode slowly down the green slope, her image reflected in the water. Her cheeks were flushed and her eyes very wide. The other riders made way for her to join Peter.

'Lucia, this is the Baron Nicholas de Menyll. The Lady Lucia le Latimer de Thweng.'

They regarded each other briefly, bowed and looked away – Lucia, to hide the intensity of her interest. Nicholas, because he had an impenetrable stare which discomfited people.

Peter said loudly:

'There's salmon trout for the morning meal at Mulgrave. Everyone is invited, even those who have already refused most ungraciously.'

'I come then,' Nicholas replied. 'Else I starve.'

HE STAYED FOR SIX DAYS, sleeping out each night and insisting on a place at the High Table nearest the open windows. His presence transformed the household almost as much as Lucia's had done. He was boisterous, full of stories, thoughtful and morose by turns. He ate enormously himself and fed his dog all the choicest pieces from every dish. The dog, named Cain, sat by his master's bench, his head well above the level of the table, for he was as large as a calf. Cain fed better than many of the villeins at the lower end of the Hall, but nobody dared murmur.

A few of the Mulgrave guests had departed hurriedly on the Baron de Menyll's arrival. Others took their places without delay. It was safest to be friendly towards a man like de Menyll, who had a finger in many pies – smuggling, poaching, financial juggling, to name but a few. He was reputed to be fantastically wealthy and nobody underestimated his influence. Even upon the Church – which he did not attend – he had a sizable hold by way of mortgages on wool, and when Nicholas himself gave banquets at Whorlton Castle, even the Superiors of enclosed Orders attended if bidden, against all the rules of their houses for none dared offend him.

This was the man Lucia wanted and needed and meant to have. Sometimes, in his quieter moods, he reminded her of her Uncle Marmaduke, and a wave of homesickness would wash over her. At other times she feared him with a deep primitive fear, knowing that his anger could be more destructive even than her own. But, through longing or fear, he fascinated her and dominated her every thought. She was a changed woman in manner and appearance.

At first, de Menyll's attention had ranged wide over the entire company, then had narrowed to the few who could hold conversation with him, laugh and think and argue with him, defy, ride out and hunt in the dark with him. Lucia was the only woman in this select company.

On the evening of the fifth day, Nicholas sought out Peter to bid him farewell privately. They retired to the deserted winter parlour.

'You have enjoyed your brief stay, Nicholas?' Peter was as anxious to be on the right side of de Menyll as anybody else: and now, also, he wanted a great favour, on the granting of which his very life depended. 'Is it vital that you return to Whorlton so soon?' he pressed.

'Aye, I thank you. Many matters await my attention.'

Peter sighed and put his head between his hands.

'I could wish that you were not leaving…'

'Why is that?'

'Lucia.'

'What of her?'

'She will be liked a caged lioness again. You gave her a breath of freedom. I am not strong enough to untether and defend her at the same time.'

After a pause, Nicholas asked:

'What will become of her eventually?'

Peter shrugged.

'The le Latimers will take her away as soon as young William returns from Scotland. I dare not stop them in defiance of the King. But, for myself, I shall be happier without her; she has proved too much for me, and I have another wench in any case. But one hates to see a splendid woman destroyed. Could you not take her to Whorlton with you, Nicholas?'

The baron started back as though charged by a boar.

'God's blood, saddle myself with a woman? You must

be out of your mind. I am a wild man, de Mauley, and Whorlton is a man's household.'

. They both meditated for a while, then de Menyll spoke again:

'I will admit she rides well. She has stamina, vitality and great intelligence. I had not thought of her as a woman until you mentioned taking her away.'

Peter gazed at him hopefully.

'She is your kind, Nicholas. You are the only man who can handle her. And remember, the northern winters are long and lonely.'

Nicholas caressed his hound's ear.

'Perhaps that is why I have delayed so long here. Something held me; the threat of loneliness?'

'No. The promise of a grown woman.'

'Would she come with me?'

'Ask her.'

He went out alone and found her on the little lawn below the ladies' balcony. The ladies knitted and embroidered, but Lucia was fiercely engaged in throwing stones into the beck. She knew that Nicholas was leaving, and she knew that she had failed altogether to impress him with her womanhood. Her company had not provoked the faintest glimmer of desire in him. Failure was doubly bitter after years of easy conquest. She flung larger stones with greater force.

'Lucia,' he called, trying to keep his voice low and not succeeding.

'Yes?'

He strode towards her.

'You are coming to Whorlton with me in the morning,' he said: a direct command was the only form of request that he knew.

The ladies on the balcony crossed themselves and bit

their underlips. Lucia stared at de Menyll. She was balancing a large stone in the palm of her hand and the idea that she might throw it at him crossed her mind. He took her hand, stone and all, in his.

'Do you agree?' he roared.

She nodded. The ladies released in unison the breaths which they had held and all began to talk at once and to scurry hither and thither, spreading the news of Cleveland's strangest, yet most inevitable, alliance.

9

Nicholas and Lucia left Mulgrave together at daybreak. She took nothing with her except her jewel-case; Peter had promised to send a wagon with her belongings when all was safe.

The wolfhound, Cain, loped ahead.

'To Danby beacon,' Nicholas said, shifting the knives in his belt so that the longest was to hand. 'We'll skirt Ugthorpe and avoid the Guisborough to Whitby road: I have no wish to lay your father-in-law in his grave before time! We'll cross the Esk where it's shallow below Westerdale Moor and then climb to the dykes on top. The stone circles there are pleasant places to pass a summer's night...'

Lucia thought of the many journeys she had made over heather, bracken and marsh and remembered hunger, weariness, and loneliness. Now, looking at the man by her side and listening to his voice, she was not afraid of any of these things. A rough comradeship had sprung up between them, like that which men and women shared when working together in the fields. Anticipation of physical nearness in the night was comforting, fraught with no qualms. Nicholas would take her as she was, with an easy animal acceptance – not with red-hot conscience as Duke had done; nor awkwardness, as William had once tried to do; nor scenting and speech-making like Peter.

She was content and at peace, an experience she had not known since the old days at Kilton when her uncle was master of the household and Friar Alan the keeper of her conscience. These two offices were now combined in Nicholas.

Soon after nightfall they reached the top of Westerdale Moor. The sky was clear and silver-blue from a huge rising moon. Long quiet clouds were moored on the horizon, their undersides still faintly flushed from sunset. It was a night of utter peace and vast distances around and above. The standing stones and hut circles of the ancient British settlement were silvered with moonlight on the one side, purple with shadow on the other. Heat mist was rising from the dales, hazing them over. Here, on the moor top, one was alone on the roof of Cleveland.

They tended the horses, fed the hound, and ate their own evening meal of freshly killed meat. Wine from a leather bottle was sweet and strong.

They lay down together.

NEXT MORNING, as they crossed Great Hograh Moor, the tinkling of a bell made them pause to look down into lonely Baysdale. There, the tiny Cistercian convent huddled among bushes and boulders, its patchwork fields climbing the sides of the dale. A brown-clad figure watched sheep in the western hollow and two other nuns, dressed in white, were digging in the kitchen garden.

'I know the Abbess of that convent,' Lucia said

suddenly. 'I used to visit her with my Aunt Isabel when the nuns lived at Hutton. Her name is Susanna.'

Nicholas grinned.

'It is unlikely that you would be welcome there now, my lady. Come.'

She followed him, still looking back. The peace and order and isolation of the little dale appealed to one side of her nature. It would be nice to see the eagle-faced Abbess again – a woman of great learning, although afflicted with poor health – to talk with her of old times, to ask for advice and comfort… With a jolt, Lucia remembered how far outside the religious circle she now stood. Nicholas was right. It was unlikely that she would be welcome. She was his mistress.

They sighted the Cross at the boundary of Cleveland and Blackamoor, and rested there, looking down on to the Tees Valley.

'What church is that, Nicholas?' Lucia asked, pointing.

'The old church of Ingleby Greenhow. Up there is Urra Moor, which we must cross. Are you rested?'

On and on they pressed, leaving Cleveland further behind.

'We are approaching the Bilsdale Pass,' Nicholas said, some hours later. 'It will be busy, and therefore dangerous. If you are recognised, I may be challenged to give you up.'

Again his hand strayed to his belt and he flicked a naked knifetip with one finger.

She smiled at him.

'He would be a foolhardy man to challenge you, Nicholas.'

His face was set, the black eyes alert.

'They do not travel alone here,' he said quietly, 'but in bands of ten or twenty.'

Suddenly she was afraid, for herself and for him also. It was the beginning of the love she was to know for him.

The Pass was deserted as they approached, but the feel of danger was everywhere – in the stiff-legged, tiptoed gait of the hound, in the backward slant of the horses' ears, in the glint of the knives, in the silence, the heat, the dust… This travelling on a low level after the height of the moors gave them a feeling of being encompassed by enemies.

They were about to enter the Pass when Nicholas's hand clamped on Lucia's shoulder and he pushed her violently; her mount swerved.

'Up there. In the bracken. Dismount. Hide.'

The bracken was shoulder high and she crouched on hands and knees, the hound pressed beside her. She heard Nicholas leading the horses away but no other sound until he came crawling towards her, breathing heavily.

'Look!' he whispered.

They peered through the bracken. The first horseman of a large party was emerging from the Pass.

'It's'—she almost shouted aloud—'Thomas le Latimer from Sinnington…'

'Aye,' Nicholas breathed, 'a great visitor is fat Thomas. There he goes with de Neville and Percy. Three of de Fauconberg's nephews follow. And old Ingleram, another self-interested Christian. Hunting, are they? No. Or on a pilgrimage maybe. More likely to spend a night of debauchery away from their own homes. Or perhaps they're searching for us; news travels fast. If my lands could be made forfeit, many of these gentlemen would be richer after a few favours to the Crown. Eh, Lucia? Did it hurt to lose Danby?'

'Oh, be quiet, Nicholas. Here come some more – nine, ten, eleven…'

'I know them not,' he said. 'Down, Cain. You tremble like a leaf, dog, whereas your mistress did not even cry out!'

'I was too frightened to make a sound,' Lucia confessed. 'Does Cain often shake like that?'

'Yes, poor fool. His kind are rare and therefore too closely bred. He is brave as a lion in the chase, but trembles before the evil intentions of man hunting man. He is an outlaw, like his master.'

The party had now passed out of sight in the direction of Urra Moor. Lucia scrambled to her feet while Nicholas went to fetch the horses. She did not fully regain her composure until they were high on Cringle and the small round hummock of the Whorl lay before and below them in the evening light. Beyond was the village and castle of Whorlton, whose Lord was coming home.

THE SUMMER of 1305 lingered far into the autumn months. Heather glowed red and purple on the moors and the heat at midday was often as great as at high summer, but the mists of early morning and late evening gave impetus to the work of preparing for winter. Nicholas was increasingly occupied with organising hunts and the laying by of stores. He marked the places where trees were to be felled. He consulted with shepherd and bailiff and clerk about the all-important sheep flocks. He rode to the furthest extent of his lands to take inventory from every tenant before mud and snow should hinder him. He dealt out swift, and often rough, justice at the Courts.

In all these activities, Lucia was his companion. For two main reasons, Whorlton accepted her: she kept its Lord at home when his presence was most needed, and her influence often sweetened his temper.

These months at Whorlton had made her superbly woman; beautiful as a healthy animal, content as a well-mated wife.

She was industrious in transforming the male atmosphere of the castle's private apartments into some semblance of comfort. Generations of de Menyll women had stored away a wealth of furs and tapestries, fine table and bed linen; these she brought out and put into use, and her greatest reward was to return from a long cold ride with Nicholas to a room bright with blazing logs, and hear him say:

'Lucia, it pleases me to come home now!'

Then, as if remembering bleak winter nights in the past, when there were no guests at Whorlton, nothing to do except pore over accounts or talk to his dog, he would take her in his arms before she had time to remove her riding coat, and kiss her cold face and hands. She was often tired or stiff from a day in the saddle, and Nicholas's loving was seldom gentle, but she never withdrew from him. To the end, she was to be grateful to him. In the end, she was to love him as few men are loved.

Yet neither submitted personality nor will to the other in the business of everyday living. The violence and waywardness of de Menyll remained undiminished, and Lucia's quarrelsome demanding nature often found a target in her lover, although it was his absence which annoyed her rather than his company. Nicholas had a habit of vanishing without warning for days or even weeks at a time. Then Lucia moped or raved or flirted as the mood took her, just as she had done at Mulgrave.

'Look, my love,' Nicholas would shout gaily on his return, 'a leather purse all the way from Cordova! I had it from a seaman at Newcastle...' Or perhaps it would be some exquisite Venetian glass, or metalware from Dinant, or cloth from Italy or Flanders. She could never hide her enthusiasm for such gifts, and laughter and love would come back into her life.

The feast of Christmas came with its twelve days of merrymaking. The Great Hall was ablaze with torch and taper, every villein, beggar, sokeman and tenant seated either on bench or floor, eating and drinking as though the end of the world were nigh. The Baron de Menyll was a hard master, but when he gave a feast he did it with the thoroughness which characterised his every undertaking.

Musicians played, but nobody heard them above the uproar. Dogs fought and were ejected. An old man's beard caught fire and a woodcutter's wife was carried to the kitchens to give birth to a child. A youth choked on a goose bone.

At the High Table, honoured guests tried to hold dignified conversation.

'Trouble between our Lord King again and his son, I hear.'

'Indeed? What is it now?'

'Something concerning Walter Langton, the Treasurer. Young Edward insulted him.'

'Poor fellow. He can do nothing right by his father. Yet I hear he's a handsome one, manly made.'

'Aye, a good enough soldier too. He has four Scottish campaigns to his credit. Nicholas, you know the young Prince of Wales. Tell us of him.'

'Huh? Oh, a non-conformer. Swims instead of jousting. Likes to sleep late in the mornings – a reasonable preference, but one which infuriates his father. Writes poetry and consorts with carters, ditchers, actors and bad Barons!'

Everybody laughed except the first speaker, who was sunk in gloom.

'They say he's more interested in how mechanical

things work than in how an army moves. I fear he'll make no King when the time comes!'

'He is little more than twenty years old,' Nicholas said shortly. 'He will learn.'

Nicholas liked the Prince of Wales and was sick of hearing gloomy prophecies concerning him. The lad had been starved of affection since the death of Eleanor of Castile, his mother; it was ill-luck which brought emotional friendship to him later in the person of Piers Gaveston rather than that of some court lady.

The last flame was extinguished on Twelfth Night, everyone had gone home or laid sleeping in the Hall, Nicholas and Lucia were in bed together in their firelit apartment, when a messenger hammered on Whorlton's gate.

Nicholas dressed and went out with the man who had been sent to summon him. A rider, still mounted, awaited him, the breaths of horse and man white in the frosty air.

'Well, what is it?' Nicholas growled.

'The Lord of Danby, William, father-in-law of the Lady Lucia, is dead.'

The gatekeeper crossed himself.

'That doesn't surpise me,' Nicholas said without reverence. 'He'll be in hell by this time. Who sent you?'

'The new Lord, the lady's husband.'

'Ah-ha!' Nicholas rubbed his high-bridged nose meditatively, and the gatekeeper thought, for the hundredth time, how like his own wolfhound the master looked. It was a subject he often raised with his wife. 'Do you not agree that the Baron looks like the hound, Cain?' 'You mustn't say things like that!' 'But don't you think so? The long, high nose, the burning eyes?' 'Well, maybe; but I don't say it. You be careful…'

Nicholas finished his reflections and shot a question at

the messenger so suddenly that the lantern jerked in the guilty gatekeeper's hand.

'Is the son prostrate with grief or frightened out of his wits, eh?'

'I – I know not, my Lord. I bring only the message which was given to me for you in person.'

'You have eyes, haven't you? Oh, find a bed with the dogs until morning.'

Nicholas strode away over the cobbled yard. Stars winked in a black sky. He tripped over a log, cursed it and whoever had left it there, and went up to the private apartments where the fire was still alight but low.

Lucia sat up, naked, in bed.

'What is it?' she shivered.

He put a rug around her.

'News which will not grieve you. Your father-in-law is dead. Young William sent the messenger.'

'Why did he do that?'

Nicholas shrugged.

'It is customary to inform one's wife when one comes into a title!'

'Do not joke, Nicholas. He has something in mind. What is your opinion?'

'That he wants you to return to him to protect the inheritance.'

She threw her arms around his neck and asked, with childish need for reassurance:

'He cannot harm us nor separate us?'

His hand caressed her under the rug and an unaccustomed sadness crept into his eyes, which made him look more than ever like Cain.

'No,' he said then, with the utter certainty which was a part of him, 'no one can do that except ourselves...'

There the matter rested for several months. Lucia sent

no message to her husband and it must have been obvious to him that she had no intention of returning. He then tried to force her hand by applying to the Consistory Court of York for a divorce.

Still there was no reaction from Whorlton.

Now young William missed the guiding influence of his late father. Under that astute parent's leadership, the divorce proceedings would most certainly have been called off, but William allowed them to go ahead, not realising the consequences.

In the end, freedom was to cost him the manors of Yarm, Brunne, Skinningrove and Brotton, all parts of Lucia's inheritance which the Kings' Escheator promptly took into royal hands.

This news convulsed Nicholas with mirth. Lucia, however, considered it quietly and then acted with great foresight.

She conveyed all the lands remaining to her to the Rector of Rudby, in trust for any children she might have by de Menyll, thus preventing her estates from descending to the youngest le Latimer, Duke's natural son. It was not that she bore the child any ill-will, but the name of le Latimer was poison to her.

Details of this legal transaction were soon noised abroad, and William, panic-stricken lest he lose any more land, now made himself look a fool indeed: he applied to the King for a letter under the Privy Seal ordering all persons to assist him recover the wife he had just applied to divorce!

The order was enrolled in the Assize Roll but nothing came of it. The combined influence of the families de Menyll, de Thweng and de Mauley saw to that, effectively.

But William le Latimer was angry and frightened. He sulked and brooded. There was nothing now which he would not do to injure the man who was the root cause of his humiliation. Urged on and taunted by his mistress, the soft-footed Mary Godwin, he concocted a scheme for revenge. Remained only to find someone to carry it out for him.

10

R obert de Bordesdeyne, a broken-down soldier, sat in
the smithy at Castleton and surveyed his horse
gloomily. The cost of the shoe now being fitted was going
to take his last penny, but the news which the farrier had
just given him was the worst blow of all: old William le
Latimer was dead since Christmas! De Bordesdeyne had
come a long way to see his former commander from the
Gascony campaign and he had travelled in certain expecta-
tion of recompense for past services.

'You say his son is now in residence at Danby Castle?'
he asked the farrier. 'What kind of a man is he?'

The farrier tried to be charitable.

'Lord William has his own troubles,' was the best he
could find to say about him.

Things could be no worse. The soldier paid the farrier,
led his horse away and rode slowly up the long hill,
debating aloud about what he ought to do. Hunger
decided him. He would see the new Lord, and embroider a
tale about the friendship that had existed between himself
and the old man.

But—

'I never heard of you,' the new Lord of Danby said flatly. 'Now get away out of here or I'll call the dogs.'

Hurt – for he already believed his own story – de Bordesdeyne regarded the fat, dirty figure that lounged on a bench in the courtyard.

'I did your father great service in France,' he said with dignity, 'but now that he is gone…' His mottled face crumpled with grief and he indicated that he, too, would depart to almost certain death from weariness and hunger.

He began to walk away, shoulders hunched, and William watched him dully. The soldier was almost out of sight now. William spat.

'Crawling liar. Sell his soul for a marc.'

Suddenly he jerked upright.

'Here,' he yelled. 'You! Come back…'

A crawling liar who would sell his soul for a marc was exactly the man he wanted.

It was late that night when they finished haggling and bargaining. Terms were agreed. Le Latimer would pay to Robert de Bordesdeyne the sum of fifty marcs and all out-of-pocket expenses if the soldier would swear that he had been engaged by Nicholas de Menyll of Whorlton to murder the Lord of Danby.

'And, if you do not do this thing, or bungle it in any way, I now have sufficient evidence against you to have you imprisoned for life.'

There was no backing out for the soldier. He had been over anxious to impress this loutish son with tales of courage and cunning, believing that very little actually penetrated the dull brain. But he had underestimated the

Lord of Danby, who had a peasant's memory for detail. Every tale of dubious, or downright criminal, transactions in the army could, William said, be checked with his father's copious diaries. Robert believed him and, panic-stricken, yelped:

'Imprisoned – for life?'

'For life,' William repeated.

'Very well.' The soldier licked his lips. 'I will take your money for this business, although the sum you offered is little enough for the serious trouble I can get into. What will happen if anything goes amiss?'

'You must not worry. Worry weakens resolution. I give you my personal undertaking that no harm shall come to you. I have much power in these parts as the Lord of great estates, and much influence with the King. The Baron de Menyll, on the other hand, is a notoriously violent man and the Justices will take a serious view of any charge brought against him. He has given them much trouble in the past.'

Uneasy, but driven by the devil, de Bordesdeyne set about his plans. He bribed a namesake of his, one Robert, son of Philip the Blacksmith of Scampston, and Thomas of Roston, to swear in court that they had been engaged by him to murder William le Latimer. One of them was to act as informer on the other so that they would both be arrested and questioned, and de Bordesdeyne brought in. And if this plan savoured of putting a rope around one's own neck, de Bordesdeyne dismissed the idea from his mind: he had absolute confidence in the Lord of Danby, son of his old commander...

Now the Justices examined de Bordesdeyne and, of course, his story corresponded exactly with the evidence of the two bribed men. Still secure in the belief that the Lord of Danby could save him from all harm, de Bordesdeyne made only a feeble attempt to minimise his own guilt.

'I was desperate, my Lords. Hungry and homeless. My terrible injuries as a soldier – received fighting your enemies, my Lords! – precluded me from active work. I went to beg bread and board from the son of my old commander; but what did he do? He sent me away hungry, cursed and spat at me, would not even allow me to water my stumbling horse at the trough!

'It was in this condition that I encountered the Baron de Menyll in Pickering Forest, and he seemed to read my thoughts, as though he were possessed by evil spirits.

' "You have a grudge against the Lord of Danby," he said to me, and I agreed for I was weak and much vexed. "So have I," he said, "and I am seeking two strong men to murder him for me. Now, if you could find such men, and hire them to do the deed, you could make much profit and live comfortably to a great age." '

The Justices, impressed, called upon le Latimer, asking him if he wished to proceed against de Menyll as the principal criminal. Le Latimer replied, emphatically, that he did, and was bound over, with two sureties, to prosecute at the next assizes.

So far, everything had gone according to plan, and Nicholas de Menyll was in a very precarious position indeed, for he was absent from Whorlton during the whole of the time when these events were supposed to have taken place and, furthermore, he had been seen in Pickering Forest by three independent witnesses.

The Justices, however, were cautious men and threw de Bordesdeyne and his two accomplices into the dungeons of York Castle to await trial. De Menyll was ordered not to leave Whorlton until he should be escorted to York at the time of the assizes.

Three weeks dragged by and William le Latimer made
no attempt to keep his promise to the old soldier, that he
should come to no harm. Half-starved and rat-bitten, de
Bordesdeyne was taken from the dungeons and brought
before the court. And now he was an angry and a disillu-
sioned man.

Turning red-rimmed eyes on William le Latimer – who
had come to hear de Menyll sentenced – he shouted:

'There is the criminal who concocted the entire
scheme!'

The full confession poured out, was checked and
counter-checked. Motive was obvious; means were apparent. A wool-broker swore that he saw de Bordesdeyne go
into Danby Castle with le Latimer's arm about his shoulders while his horse was attended to by le Latimer's
groom…

'We find the Baron de Menyll guiltless,' was the verdict
of the court, which now turned its terrible gaze upon the
Lord of Danby and demanded several explanations
from him…

LUCIA'S RELIEF at the vindication of her lover was overwhelming. All through the trial period she had been in an
agony of guilt, knowing that she herself had concentrated
the enmity of le Latimer upon Nicholas. Now he was
home, safe by her side, it seemed as if the trouble they had
shared had deepened the love between them.

At any rate, Nicholas took no more trips abroad on
smuggling expeditions: he paid his wool taxes and duties
like an honest man and only continued to poach the King's
lands. For Nicholas, this was indeed reformation.

Lucia now considered that the time was ripe to make a

public announcement of her pregnancy (that same which had prompted her to convey her lands to the Rector of Rudby, and which had, indirectly, begotten the murder plot). She made her condition known by engaging two nurses and a seamstress, all three chosen with infinite care. The senior nurse – a fat, white-haired old woman with bad feet and a chuckling laugh – had reared Nicholas and was therefore an obvious choice; but she needed an assistant, and Lucia was wary of younger women, remembering Mary Godwin. However, in the end she chose a girl of fifteen whose thick fair hair, worn loose to her waist, proclaimed her unmarried state. This girl had smooth brown skin, slow brown eyes and large hands. The parish had christened her Christina when she was thrown upon its mercies at birth: her mother had been beaten soundly at the Cross for bringing this burden upon the people...

The seamstress was a cripple and middle-aged and foul tempered. She expressed her wrath against her own ugliness by working at three times the speed of an ordinary woman, and never lifting her eyes from the cloth which she sewed, even when addressed by her mistress.

It now appeared that the Whorlton ménage was almost on a matrimonial footing. There was nothing to hinder the marriage of either party – for the divorce had been granted to le Latimer by the Consistory Court of York – and Lucia secretly wished for such a consummation, if only to legitimise the unborn child.

But the idea of matrimony, at which Nicholas had shied all his life, did not commend itself to him now either. He had chosen Lucia because she was as lawless as himself, as freedom-loving and as unwilling to be shackled by the Church: he could not imagine why the bearing of a child should alter her mind, but he put it down to a temporary disturbance due to pregnancy. If he married her now, he argued furiously with himself, she would hold it against him from the moment her body – and therefore, according to him, her mind – returned to normal.

He constituted himself her protector against this strange derangement and no force on earth would induce him to marry her, although many forces were brought to bear upon him. One was an emissary from Anthony Bek, Bishop of Durham and Patriarch of Jerusalem.

'Dire consequences,' intoned the messenger-monk, 'will result if ye continue to flout God's law and scandalise the flock.'

'I suppose his Lordship is holding excommunication over our heads?' Nicholas asked mildly.

'Not yet,' the monk replied. 'He awaits the birth of the child, trusting that God's miracle will transform ye.'

'Tell him, then, that he may baptise my son – the christening feast will be worth attending. But there will be no wedding either before or after. I am a wild man and my Lord Bishop a turbulent one. He will understand, having made his token protest.'

Sadly, the monk shuffled away, praying aloud for all sinners.

LUCIA LAY IN SNOWY LINEN, the child on her breast, the old nurse nodding quietly in a chair after her exertions in delivering the newborn. Young Christina was on her knees in prayer of gratitude and joy, as though before the Christmas manger; she had never seen a child born before and was speechless with wonder.

It was dark outside now and many people had gathered in the courtyard below, waiting for confirmation of the news.

'It's a boy!' Lucia had heard them shout. Then somebody else said, no it was a girl or twins…

She was glad that Nicholas had a son. He had never doubted the sex of the child from the time of its conception.

She felt him bending over her now, taking the new life out of her arms. She saw the nurse wrap it in a shawl, saw Nicholas carry it to the unshuttered window, heard the pride in his voice as he announced to his people:

'This is my son, to be called Nicholas, who will one day be the Baron de Menyll and heir to all my estates.'

'Bend sinister be damned,' he added, as the people cheered and he turned away from the window. 'You have done well, my lady.'

'And you have done well by my son, Nicholas, acknowledging him at once as your heir. Neither of us has any claims upon your estate…'

HISTORY MARCHED with the old King as he set his face once more towards Scotland. Since early spring the Bruce had gathered an increasing army about him, and now he defeated the Royal captains, Valence and young Gloucester, and shut the latter up in Ayr Castle.

Edward summoned fresh troops to Carlisle and determined to ride once more at their head, although he was weak and ill.

His last official act before quitting London had been to forbid the citizens to annoy his second wife, Margaret, by burning fires near the Tower. But relations with his grown children were never put right: he had torn out masses of his son's hair, enraged by the young man's request that the country of Ponthieu should be conferred on Piers Gave-

ston: he had flung his daughter's coronet into the fire
during a violent quarrel with her, causing the loss of a
great ruby and a great emerald.

This Edward was not the same man who had followed
the body of Eleanor of Castile, his first wife, on foot, to its
last resting place, causing crosses to be erected everywhere
the cortège stopped on its journey. This was not the man
who had paid ten shillings and fourpence out of his own
purse 'for a little painted boat for my son, Alfonzo'.
Alfonzo was the princeling who was to die a few months
later leaving his brother, Edward, to take his place. This
Edward never succeeded in doing right as far as his father
was concerned. The great brain which had fathered the
laws of England was to perish in rage and failure, leaving
not a vestige of affectionate memory with the man who
would wear his crown.

Wracked by dysentery, Edward quitted Carlisle on
Monday, the third of July, 1307. On the following day he
rode only two miles, and on the Wednesday was unable to
move at all.

'I shall die soon,' he said, resigned.

Then, with great force:

'We direct that our dead body shall accompany the
army until the final conquest of Scotland.'

They carried him to Burgh-on-Sands, humouring
him, telling him he was better; but, as attendants lifted
him up to take his honoured place at table, the King
died.

Not without reason, his last wishes were disregarded:
the conquest of Scotland was far more remote than
Edward dreamed. His body was taken, first, to Waltham
Abbey, and thence to Westminster, where it lies under a
simple tomb, inscribed in Latin:

*Here lies Edward the First, the Hammer of the
Scots. Thirteen hundred and seven. Keep troth.*

But it was as Edward the Lawgiver that he was to be
remembered with pride.

IN THE FOLLOWING FEBRUARY, the new King was crowned.

Nicholas journeyed to London for the event in
company with Peter de Mauley, the de Thweng menfolk,
Nevilles, Percys and a host of others who would swear allegiance on bended knee, whatever their misgivings.

It was almost thirty-four years since there had been a
coronation, and Lucia was as impatient as any other
woman to hear every detail of it from her returning lord.
But Nicholas was morose and withdrawn until after the
evening meal when, warmed by wine and company, he
burst forth—

'It was Gaveston who offended. He carried St.
Edward's Crown and walked in front of the new king. Very
well. He had been chosen to do so – a tactless choice in my
opinion but openly made. Now tradition demands that
such an office shall be clothed in cloth-of-gold. But, shall I
tell you what smirking, strutting Piers wore? Purple and
pearls... *purple and pearls!* He outshone the King. Worse, he
outshone the beauty of the Queen. Every eye was upon
him. That peacock will make trouble yet for Edward of
Caernarvon.'

There was a troubled silence among the guests at the
crowded High Table.

'Tell me what the Queen looks like,' Lucia pleaded.

'Isabella? She is beautiful as a child is beautiful; there is
little of real woman in her. Her hair is fair and fine and

curling, her skin like the petals of a creamy rose. She has a dimple in her chin; her nose is tilted at the tip and her mouth is soft and pouting. She has wide blue eyes under arched brows. Her chin is rounded and her body well shaped.' Isabella was only twelve years old at the Coronation.

The company nodded agreement at this description, except for one old knight who was still pondering something else.

'Edward of Caernarvon...' he mumbled. 'Nicholas, remember the day we journeyed together to Nettleham?'

'Aye,' de Menyll, said, his expression softening, 'from the Chapter House of Lincoln Cathedral where Parliament met that year.'

'What happened at Nettleham?' Lucia asked, curious.

'The late King,' said the old knight slowly, 'sealed the Charter making his son the first English Prince of Wales. Later he was presented at Caernarvon. They say that he stood in Queen Eleanor's gateway in surcoat, cloak and mantle of crimson velvet, with a coronet on his head as token of principality; in his hand, a verge of gold, the emblem of government; on his middle finger, a ring of gold. And the people loved him because he was handsome as an archangel, and proud. And because he was their Prince.'

Tears sprang to Lucia's eyes, as often happened when beauty appeared to her in any form, especially beauty which was threatened. Piers Gaveston was the threat to the King.

Soon, disturbing tales began to circulate throughout the country. Gaveston's capers at the coronation had brought the wrath of the Queen not only upon his own head but upon the head of Edward also. The royal pair had not been long married, but there was enmity between them, the cause of which was Edward's affection for Gaveston. Now, Edward had not wanted to marry anybody, not even Isabella *'la plus belle la rose'*, but he was willing to be philosophical about the necessity provided it did not interfere with his friendship with Gaveston. Gaveston was the one person who had brought love – even perverted love – into Edward's love-starved life. Gaveston was as clever, outrageous as all the other nobles were dull, and Edward could not live without his company. The worst possible construction was put upon the relationship.

For a long time Edward tried to placate his Queen, but in the end, theatrical-minded as ever, he took to carrying a knife in his hose 'to kill Isabella; and if I had no weapon, I would crush her with my teeth!'

This was the standard of kingship which Edward set, a standard perilously low. Yet, one day, he was to faint with grief and shock at the extent of his subjects' disloyalty.

11

Lucia was sitting on the floor, playing with her eighteen-month-old son. Loud shrieks proclaimed the success of the game, which involved a wooden bear, covered in fur, his open jaws lacquered red, advancing on young Nicholas and being snatched away just in time by Lucia. Whorlton's heir was not alarmed by this familiar enemy. Indeed, he slept with it at night, his black curls and holly-red cheeks pressed against the furry chest.

Already his father had acquired a set of war-like puppets for the child. Fully clothed in armour, they could be manipulated into fighting positions and made to strike each other with a resounding clang.

Nicholas senior lost no opportunity to see that his son inherited his own qualities. A pony had been specially bred for the infant's first riding lessons. The old nurse was bribed to bathe him in cold water during the summer months. He had cut his first tooth on the carved and diamond-studded hilt of the baron's sheathed hunting dagger.

And Lucia was as proud of this child as she had been

ashamed and impatient of her first. Young Nicholas was as strong as a bull calf: uncomplaining if he fell; intelligent in observation and mimicry; passionately loving, but independent of the women who tended him. He was all she had ever wanted a son of hers to be except, perhaps, legitimate.

She often dreamed of what a splendid man he would grow to be, and she wondered, jealously, whom he would wed. But her imagination did not extend to his children, her own grandchildren. If it had, she might have seen, as in a vision, a young woman called Elizabeth, her own image, married to Lord Peter de Mauley the Sixth of Mulgrave, son of Lucia's former lover...

The game with the bear was interrupted by Christina, the young nurse.

'My lady, there is a nun who wishes to speak with you. She says her name would be unknown to you.'

Lucia straightened her cross-gartered hose, bound up the long brown hair which young Nicholas had pulled loose, and brushed the floor dust off her dress. She did not hurry. Doubtless the nun was either begging or preaching salvation.

'Where have you put her, Christina?'

'In the winter parlour, my lady.'

'Take care of Nicholas...'

The young nun was dressed in brown. Layers of white dust marked her skirt up almost to the girdle, and her hands were calloused like a farm labourer's. When she spoke, her voice had the tone of a voice seldom used.

'I come from Baysdale, my lady. Our Abbess, Susanna, is sick and begs that you visit her.'

Lucia was astonished. How did Susanna, cut off from the world in her Cistercian remoteness, know that Lucia was at Whorlton? A visiting cleric would have told her, perhaps. But then, he would have told her much else besides: why, therefore, should Susanna seek the company of such a notorious sinner? The Abbess was a woman of rigid moral standards, as befitted her position, and strict adherence to her Rule: the Rule laid down that no unnecessary outside contacts were to be made. Therefore, it must be necessary for her to see Lucia. Why? To give advice? To rant against the way of life at Whorlton and the heir's upbringing? It was possible. Many religious people had interested themselves in the situation.

'I cannot go,' Lucia told the lay-sister promptly.

She saw the rough hands tighten their clasp of the cross in the dusty lap, saw the pathetic, broken nails whiten with pressure.

'I *pray* that you will see our Abbess, my lady. Were she not ill, she would have come to you herself.'

The Abbess leave her own walls? It was unheard of.

'Well, then, you must tell me what she wants,' Lucia said. 'I cannot embark on what might be a wild-goose chase. What is it she wishes to speak to me about?'

The nun moistened her lips.

'She did not tell me.' Colour came and went in her face as conscience recognised half a lie.

Lucia studied her carefully.

'You are very distressed, sister,' she said. 'You have been told to bring me to Baysdale at all costs, is that not so?'

An eager nod.

'And now I have said that I will not come unless you give me some inkling of what is afoot. Your Abbess has instructed you with only a bare message. If you know no more, then your mission has failed. But do not think that even silent women can live together without exchanging the day's gossip in some manner. Now, what is it about which Baysdale gossips?'

The nun's eyes overflowed with tears and she fell on her knees.

'My lady, the community is in great distress. Only our Abbess knows the details of it and she has borne it all alone for a long time. Now she is sick and fears to die, leaving this trouble to her successor. She needs your help.'

Lucia breathed a deep sigh of relief.

'I will come,' she said.

Nicholas was away, and she was glad, for once, that he was. He would certainly have tried to prevent her going to Baysdale. As she dressed, she smiled to herself, remembering his views on enclosed Orders.'

'Self-interested Christians,' he would say. 'They shut themselves away from the world until something goes wrong – with *them*, not with the world – then messages pour forth from convent and monastery, "Come and help us, you whom we ignore at all other times!' They do not tend the sick nor instruct the ignorant. Their one concern is the salvation of their own smug souls.'

She had argued with him often.

'Nicholas, they pray for the world. They contemplate the Godhead which the world is too busy even to remember, although it was created for the adoration of God. The lives of the enclosed ones are harder than those of the poorest serfs, and they have chosen poverty and hardship of their own free will; they were not born to it—'

'I do not believe in their poverty. It is said that they surround themselves with luxury which is stored away when anyone visits them, and taken out again as soon as he is gone.'

'Nicholas,' Lucia had said patiently more than once, 'I never saw the slightest sign of comfort in the Cistercian house at Hutton.'

The building was smaller even than it had looked from

the moor-top on that morning three years previously, and the land on which it stood was poor. Silent white and brown clad figures working outside averted their faces as Lucia rode by.

The messenger nun led her inside. Cells opened off a narrow earth-floored passage where one walked with head bowed. Roughly carved in stone along one wall were the words, in Latin:

Soon it will be eternity.

Those words were the strength behind a life of intolerable hardship.

At the far end of the passage the nun stopped, nodded towards an opening, smiled and was gone.

Lucia found the Abbess Susanna lying flat on her back under a patched grey blanket which accentuated rather than hid the tall, spare frame underneath. Her head was bound in white linen. The skin of her face was so tightly drawn that it shone with a waxy pallor.

Susanna opened her eyes and they were as icy blue as Lucia remembered them from twenty years previously. The voice, too, when it spoke, was unaltered: a clear, incisive voice which left no doubt about the mind of the speaker being one trained to set words in order, sparingly but with force.

'It was kind of you to come, Lucia. Let me look at you.'

Like a small girl again, Lucia moved obediently over to the narrow bed.

'Hmmm,' Susanna said, ' "the Helen of Cleveland", I hear. Well, well. I know little about ships but a great deal about the fences you have tampered with…'

Lucia felt a sudden colour rising in her face, but could still think of nothing to say except:

'I – I hope you are better.'

'I am not better. I fall down when I try to walk.

However, my health is not the subject we wish to discuss. Nor your morals. Sit down, child.'

Lucia looked in vain for somewhere to sit. The cell was quite bare of furniture. Susanna patted the bed impatiently with her long, thin hand. When Lucia sat on the bed, she realised that it was a wooden plank, covered only by the one wretched blanket that lay on top of the Abbess. There was no undercover of any kind.

'I will make my confession now,' Susanna said in a businesslike manner, 'about my worldly and financial failings; the spiritual ones can wait. Are you tired or hungry or thirsty?'

Lucia was all three, but in the face of the Abbess's discomfort on the wooden plank, shook her head vigorously.

'Very well,' Susanna said, as though that was the answer she had anticipated. 'As you will have heard, we moved here from Hutton eight years ago. There were thirteen of us then. We moved in the early summer and slept outside while we built this house with our own hands. I used the dowries of the three youngest sisters to finance the move and the building, and to buy more sheep for cross-breeding.

'Two sisters died that autumn. One fell dead suddenly while digging a ditch; the other lingered many weeks, coughing blood.

'In the following three winters, we lost sheep in snow, lambs had their eyes pecked out by starving birds, ewes were sterile when the spring came. I spent another dowry in replenishing the flock and things improved generally. The following spring we sold a great deal of wool, but, later, we had a bad harvest. And I lost another lay-sister.

'Now, nobody denies that the Cistercian death-rate is high. I have seen strong young women fade away in a few years from sleeplessness, abstinence, cold and overwork, but they could usually be saved, even at the eleventh hour, by a course of opposites: rest and warmth and good food. Now, however, when my daughters took ill, I had nothing to give them, and the deaths weighed heavily upon my conscience... but not more heavily than the loss of dear children upon my heart. I am so old, you see, and so wise. They were young girls who had exchanged their mothers for me, and I led them out of pleasant, wooded Hutton into this wilderness, telling them that life here was more in keeping with the Cistercian concept.'

The Abbess lay silent, looking upward, the skin taut and gleaming over nose and forehead, cheek and chin. She reminded Lucia of a once-splendid eagle now too weak to defend her young.

'So,' Susanna went on, 'I mortgaged the wool for twenty years.'

Lucia nodded slowly. She knew all about this system from Nicholas: a lump sum was paid to a House in exchange for five or ten or twenty years' wool from a certain number of sheep. The practice had brought ruin to many borrowers.

'I am a mathematician,' Susanna continued bitterly, 'but I was guilty of a gross miscalculation.'

'How was that?'

'By leaving too fine a margin for our own use. For two years now we have had no wool for ourselves.'

Lucia looked at the blanket, then at a white habit hanging against the bare wall. Both were thin and patched and darned. Susanna's clear blue eyes followed the direction of her gaze.

'Next year,' she said, 'there will be nothing with which to patch and darn. There will be no Communion bread baked, no repairs carried out, no Papal taxes paid, no fires lit. My daughters will die here in the winter months. There are only seven left. And myself. It was my folly and bad leadership which brought the House to this pass. I decided to break my Rule to ask for your help. Also, to risk your refusal.'

'I will not refuse,' Lucia said quietly. 'Tell me what must be done and I will do it. But on my own terms.'

The ice-blue eyes bored into the glowing brown ones.

'I am accustomed to harsh terms,' Susanna replied without self-pity. 'What are yours?'

'That I may find a refuge here if and when I need one.'

She never knew why she said the words, or from whence the idea came. But, all at once, she knew that she had a home behind her for the first time since leaving Kilton.

It was the child's second birthday and he was allowed to come to the High Table for the evening meal. The bench between Nicholas and Lucia was padded high with cushions for him to sit upon. All heads turned to watch him, his black curly head on a level with the great salt-cellar, his diminutive scarlet tunic looking like a shield on the chest of the dog, Cain, which sat protectively behind him.

Young Nicholas had been well trained in the nursery and fed himself, unattended, except when his father leaned over to cut his meat for him.

Lucia, watching them as she ate, experienced a coldness around the heart, a sense of being no longer necessary, which many mothers feel when they cease to feed a child themselves. He was Nicholas's son now, not hers, and Nicholas was content with an only child: he would not ask her to bear him another. Therefore, to him also, she was unnecessary. All the comfort and security which had lapped around her since early pregnancy vanished in that one moment while father and son ate contentedly together, feeding their dog with scraps.

'Nicholas?' Lucia said.

They both turned and looked at her enquiringly; two dark heads, two pairs of intensely alert eyes, two high-bridged noses.

'Nicholas, I must go to Kilton. Soon.'

'Kilton? Why?'

She did not know, and her gaze faltered before the combined de Menyll stare. Her old home had suddenly called to her, insistent as a bell, offering the close ties of blood and memory in brief exchange for all that Whorlton had to offer. And what had Whorlton for her now? Emptiness. Exclusion.

'I – I have a feeling that I should go. It is nearly four years since I last saw Marmaduke and Isabel and my cousins…' Her voice trailed off.

'Oh, if you wish,' Nicholas said then. 'I have business near Guisborough soon, so that I could ride most of the way with you. No, do not be alarmed. I shall not embarrass Kilton with my company!'

She laughed and put an arm about her son, and he snuggled into the sleeve of her gown. Love flowed towards her again. The moment of isolation was forgotten, but now she was committed to visiting Kilton, and for no very good reason.

FOR THE LAST few hours of the journey she was alone. It was still early afternoon, and the spring day was clear and delicate, yet she rode with increasing haste and apprehension. Something called her to Kilton, now, without delay: hurry, *hurry…*

Deliberately, she slowed her horse, forced herself to observe the remembered approaches: there was the mound of Freeborough, there was a glimpse of the North Sea; there the glint of Kilton Beck, still wild from its high moorland home. After a few miles it would drop into the beautiful ravine below the Castle.

Traces of snow still lingered in sheltered places, or where rocks' shadows barred the sun high above sea level. She had dreamed of one such place only last night. She was standing on a rock in a high, cold, desolate place. Coldness as of marble numbed her feet so that she could not move. A black wind blew out from the land, tearing her clothing from her until there was nothing left except a few shreds grasped in her hands.

Shivering, she had awakened to find that a shutter was partly open at the window of the inn where she slept with Nicholas. And Nicholas had rolled himself securely in the bed-coverings, leaving her unclothed…

She reached Kilton Castle just one hour before her Aunt Isabel died. Isabel did not recognise Lucia, although she had been ill only a few days, but her soft, plump hand sought the firm brown one of her niece and held it tightly until death loosened the grip. Then Lucia put her head down on the familiar bed and wept as though her heart would break.

It was a bitter blow to the house, this sudden passing of the mistress, but to Marmaduke it was the end of all hope, all striving, all desire to live. From that day on, he was never to look to the future for any happiness; his pleasures lay in the past.

Members of the family, hastily summoned, continued to arrive far into the night. Nobody went to bed. When all his children, and Lucia, were assembled, Marmaduke rose stiffly to his feet and spoke tonelessly.

'William, you are my eldest surviving son. I give this Castle of Kilton to you, and to your wife Catherine. See that you maintain the old traditions and care for your tenants.'

Then he sat down again, staring dully at the floor.

'Uncle,' Lucia said, putting a hand on his knee, 'where are you going to live?' It was a question she had never anticipated having to ask.

'Live? Oh, at Thwing, possibly. The manor house there is empty. But you must continue to regard Kilton as your home, Lucia.'

William and Catherine endorsed this heartily, but when their eyes met Lucia's, they found no spark of the gaiety they had once known there. Lucia was a woman gazing, horror-struck, on the ruin of an establishment which she had always considered permanent. Isabel had been mother to her, the focal point of home, and her death was an inestimable loss. But Marmaduke's departure from Kilton was the tearing up of the hearthstone.

Young and handsome, and childless, William and Catherine would not grieve for long...

The funeral ceremony brought a multitude of people to Guisborough, and the wide street leading to the Priory gates was thronged with horses and wagons and people on foot.

Lucia rode at her uncle's side, and they were greeted by representatives of all Cleveland's leading families, but there was much whispering after Lucia had passed by and some of it she overheard.

'Come back, has she? Seeking another mate...'

'They says she has three children by the murderous de Menyll!'

'The Church ought to act.'

Rumour and antagonism were a solid wall around her. Strange that here, in the capital of Cleveland, there should be such bitterness against an act which troubled Whorlton scarcely at all.

She was trembling now. She looked to her uncle for reassurance, but his eyes were looking inward and his ears were stoppered by grief. It was only his unoccupied body which rode slowly beside her past the Market Cross. She was alone in a hostile crowd. Even her beauty had deserted her after two nights of sleepless weeping.

Isabel's remains were interred in the north aisle of the chancel of Guisborough Priory. The final prayers were said. Mourners and friends began to move away, but Lucia still knelt, unnoticed.

A man stood beside her and, when she raised her head, she saw that he was a stranger. His hair was the colour of ripe beech leaves and his skin was deeply tanned by a foreign sun. His tunic bore the rust marks of armour.

He bowed to her.

'I have missed the ceremony and the mourners,' he said quietly, 'to whom I wished to offer condolence. But, by your grief and your appearance, my lady, are you not also of the family de Thweng'

'I am Lucia de Thweng. The Lady Isabel was my aunt and the wife of my guardian.'

'Accept my sympathy, my lady. I am Robert de Everingham, lately returned from abroad.'

She did not know anything of him or of his family, and it was obvious that her name conveyed nothing to him. It was comforting to meet a total stranger, one to whom her name was like any other name, untarnished, empty of implication.

She walked outside with him to where the horses were

tethered by the Priory gate. Already the Kilton party was moving away. They had not missed her and she decided not to rejoin them.

'May I escort you to wherever it is you are going, my lady?'

She studied him in silence for a moment, looking down at him from the height of her mount. He was a well-made man with honest grey eyes.

'I think it would be better for your reputation, Sir Robert de Everingham,' she said bitterly, 'if you were not seen with me in Guisborough.'

She spurred her horse and galloped out of the town in search of Nicholas, but de Everingham stood at the Priory gates for a long time, looking down the now deserted street.

12

L ucia's brief appearance in the capital had stirred up a hornet's nest. Incidents long forgotten were raked out, rumour was piled upon rumour about her life at Whorlton. Finally, the scandalised wives of Guisborough and surrounding districts incited their spouses to form a delegation to the newly-appointed Archbishop Greenfield of York, and the leader they chose was William le Latimer of Danby, Lucia's former husband.

His Grace the Archbishop of York was a small, quiet man with gently waving greyish-brown hair. When sitting in public he usually tucked his feet away out of sight under his robes, placed his hands palms downward on his knees and fixed his gaze on the great episcopal ring, as though wondering how it came to be on his finger. Many other people wondered the same thing, on first acquaintance, and some took liberties: these, however, they never repeated, for His Grace had the memory of an elephant, the eye of a hawk and the tongue of an adder.

The members of the delegation filed past him now, and each kissed the ring. His Grace studied the material of which their coats were made, and estimated its worth and usage with swift mathematical precision. Hmmm. Burgesses… landowners and merchants … a knight or two.

'Be seated,' he said mildly.

They arranged themselves in a semi-circle on the polished benches.

'Now, about the Lady Lucia de Thweng?' Greenfield prompted.

Le Latimer, the spokesman, stood up and unrolled a document.

'Your Grace, it is our opinion that this woman should be defamed throughout the Church for repeated adultery and unchastity. She is a living example of evil going unpunished. Many foolish people admire her and no man is safe from her. Is she to be allowed to breed more bastards?'

He handed over the document which listed Lucia's crimes in neat chronological order. The Archbishop glanced at it briefly.

'Judgement comes after death, not before,' he said quietly.

'We do not seek judgement, only the cessation of bad example.'

Now Greenfield transferred his gaze from the great ring to the faces of the delegation and probed each one with deliberate calm.

' "Let him who is without sin among you cast the first stone",' he quoted.

Le Latimer, being the least sensitive, replied:

'If Your Grace would complete the quotation, it is "Go, sin no more."'

Now the Archbishop smiled warmly.

'I am gratified to know that you read Holy Scripture, Sir William. You must forgive me for thinking, that day in court during the de Bordesdeyne scandal, that you were utterly ignorant of the Word of Christ…'

The Lord of Danby made a choking sound, tried to speak and brought a fit of coughing upon himself. His Grace waited politely for the noise to subside, then gave his attention to the next man on the bench.

'Ah, Thomas Thornborrow! We have met before——'

'I think not, Your Grace.'

'——When you were nearly lynched in the market place here, almost ten years ago, for using false weights and ran to my house for protection.'

'Such a thing never happened!' Thornborrow shouted, but his neighbours quietened him and then moved, significantly, away.

Greenfield was now working systematically through their ranks.

'Surely that is Guy Peacock I observe?' his pleasant voice went on. Peacock shot out of his seat and bolted through the door. The Archbishop stared after him in wonderment.

'I owe that man a marc,' he said, 'for work more thoroughly done than agreed. Does he always fly from his debtors?'

The delegation laughed uneasily while two other members – whom the Archbishop did not know from Adam – left hurriedly. Greenfield, however, was now deep in thought. He re-read the accusations against Lucia de Thweng and he knew that most of them were true. Action might have been taken sooner had she not been a great heiress with powerful connections: this was the most regrettable truth of all. But the men sitting before him also represented a large and influential community; they could no longer be ignored, nor the womenfolk who had sent them.

'I will set in motion the instrument of defamation,' he said, rising.

∾

IF SIR ROBERT DE EVERINGHAM had never heard of Lucia de Thweng before the day of the funeral in Guisborough Priory, he was destined to hear much about her afterwards. From every pulpit in the diocese the indictment thundered. People who had been in no previous danger of contamination by her example now marvelled at the complexity of her transgressions – details of which had been kept from them until now – and the 'Helen of Cleveland' legend grew apace. Young men could not sleep at nights for thinking of her, and young women wished that they could change their mates with the same ease as she had done.

Altogether, there was a good deal of unrest. Everybody knew that this roll of drums was the prelude to excommunication, if the sinner did not repent. It was difficult to imagine Lucia de Thweng wearing sackcloth.

Bets were also taken on the issue of whether de Menyll would now marry her, but close friends of the baron's did not gamble on it; they already knew his views.

'I, Nicholas de Menyll, will not be bullied, threatened nor cajoled into making any agreement. If and when I wish to marry, I will do so – but not by the direction of any bishop.'

It was an accepted fact at Whorlton that Nicholas would never relinquish this stand on principle, whatever his feelings for Lucia. That he loved her, nobody – least of all Lucia herself – doubted. That he regretted his obstinate stand, many people suspected, but he would not now give way to the Church although he flinched at the punishment which was being heaped upon Lucia. She could no longer travel outside the boundaries of Whorlton without fear of public insult, and her name was bandied about every alehouse in Cleveland and Blackamoor.

When she looked at him, he thought he read the words in her eyes:

'This is all your doing, de Menyll.'

In the end he admitted it, but only to her, alone.

'Lucia, I should have married you before our son was born. You wanted that, did you not? I was wrong to have delayed. Now it is too late.'

She made one final bid to save the situation.

'It is not too late, Nicholas—'

He rounded on her, shouting, his eyes mad.

'Is the wild man to be tamed by bald-headed clerics?'

She backed away from him startled.

'Lucia – Lucia, come here. I am sorry. But look – could you stand at the altar beside me now, watch the satisfaction on the priest's smug face, hear the people say that de Menyll had been defeated at last? Could you?'

Now her patience snapped finally.

'Stupid, selfish, insensitive animal,' she shouted, 'does nothing matter except de Menyll and his pride? Can he not control his people except by pretending to be invincible? You are weaker than a day-old kitten, more brainless than a cackling hen. I want no more of you—'

She tried to run past him and he grasped her by the shoulders. When she could not shake off his grip, she turned her head and bit him in the forearm, drawing blood.

They had had many quarrels in the past but physical violence had not entered into them, except in the love-making which followed. Neither had they tried to undermine each other's dignity and self-esteem. They did that now, with bitter unforgettable words, and each one shrank in the other's estimation with every verbal blow.

This quarrel placed the Castle of Whorlton in a state of siege. During the hours which it raged, no meal was served and retainers crept about, at once stopping their ears and trying not to miss a word. Nicholas and Lucia followed each other from room to room and everyone scurried out of their way. Christina carried young Nicholas down into the village for safety, lest he hear his parents' terrible words, and the wolfhound, Cain, crouched trembling under his master's bed; for human strife was the only thing he feared.

At last, exhausted, incoherent, leaving a trail of childish destruction behind, the two people whom nobody could harm or separate destroyed utterly the love which they had built together.

Shuddering with revulsion, Lucia rode out of Whorlton's gates.

SIR ROBERT DE EVERINGHAM was on his way to Thwing. It was the month of June. The sky was brilliant above the fresh-leaved trees and every bird in Cleveland seemed to be singing. But there was no song in the knight's heart. All he heard as he rode along were priests' voices intoning, village voices gossiping, High Table voices uproariously recalling the misdeeds of the Lady Lucia de Thweng. And he was both puzzled and troubled because her image was clear in his mind and he could not reconcile it with what was being said of her. The woman of the Priory funeral day was no wanton, he would take his oath on that. She had dignity, serenity, composure; she had womanliness enough to weep the beauty from her face for a dead relative; she had honesty and courage. But did these qualities make her any less a whore? Reason said no, they did not. It was the heart which tried to find excuses for her.

It was Sir Robert's heart, not his head, which was driving him on to visit Marmaduke de Thweng.

The manor house at Thwing was still in a state of turmoil after its lord's arrival from Kilton. Furniture was piled in the courtyard, carpenters and stonemasons sawed and chiselled and hammered, servants scurried about, seeking things – or other servants – lost, and dense clouds of black smoke issued from the kitchens.

Like a rock in a troubled sea, Marmaduke towered above the uproar, hands clasped behind his back, apparently studying a cloud high overhead.

Sir Robert begged the favour of a brief interview and they went indoors together, to a small private apartment.

'It concerns the Lady Lucia de Thweng,' Robert said earnestly.

Marmaduke nodded. He knew that it was he who should take the initiative in any action on her behalf, but he was tired, only half alive, since Isabel's death. There was no fight left in him for anyone, even for Lucia.

'Yes?' he said, without interest.

'I – I want to know the truth concerning these accusations which have been made against her.'

'They are all true.'

'Everything?'

'Everything.'

'I thank you, Sir. I will take my leave.'

The brevity of the conversation startled Marmaduke into awareness. Suddenly he was the genial host of Kilton again. His guest must stay for the evening meal – at least, for whatever part of it that was not burnt to a cinder. His horse must be attended to before he resumed his journey.

'Come, come,' Marmaduke shouted. 'I have few friends here. I have forgotten how to talk or how to listen. Tell me about your travels abroad, young man.'

Robert's shoulder was grasped in a huge hand and the mighty charm of de Thweng turned full upon him. He did not want to stay. His very soul was sick within him. Even the denial of one accusation would have given him a standard under which to fight: now, there was nothing. He wanted to go away all alone into the forest.

'I pray that you will excuse me——' But already Marmaduke was bellowing orders to cooks and grooms, and all was confusion again.

Wearily, Sir Robert sat down.

But that night, at Thwing, he found his standard. When darkness fell at last and the hammering and thumping of workmen ceased and servants settled down to quieter occupations, Marmaduke talked of the old days at Kilton with nostalgia and regret.

'It was wrong what we did, allowing the le Latimer marriage. We should have fought against it. Lucia was the only one who revolted – she and Duke. They took the one desperate course open to them... Poor children. Poor children.'

Now the pieces fell into place. The wife who deserted her husband and child the first time was a girl of sixteen, lost on the moors, raving with fever, searching for home. The wife who ran away the second time was a woman driven out by her husband's mistress. Why did she go to Mulgrave? Because Peter de Mauley had been a boyhood friend of Duke's. Again, the search for the associations of home. And why did she leave Peter for Baron de Menyll? Because he was the missing father-figure, the only one strong enough to protect her from the le Latimers and the wrath of the King...

Elation surged in de Everingham's breast.

'Sir, we can save her. By compurgation!'

Marmaduke regarded him dubiously.

'Oath-help? I do not think so. The method is full of abuses and has fallen from favour this hundred years or more.'

Nay, pardon the contradiction: it is still used inside the Church. On a charge like this, oath-witnesses of good character can secure a reprieve. We must draw up a document. I will ride with it to every castle and manor in the diocese of York and secure signatures and promises of attendance at any trial.'

THE KNIGHT who rode into York almost a month later was barely recognisable as Sir Robert de Everingham. He was thin to the point of emaciation; his splendid red-brown hair was white with dust and the clear grey eyes dulled by weariness. Since leaving Thwing manor he had ridden hundreds of miles, mostly by night. His days had been spent in pleading and argument. He had met with rebuffs and bitter disappointments, suspicion and ridicule. But he had accomplished his task to the best of his ability: the document, drawn up at Thwing, and signed by Marmaduke, now bore a list of other signatures and seals impressive enough to sway any Archbishop.

Robert carried this document inside his tunic and rode with one hand upon it at all times. His sword clanked six inches below and he wore a dagger in his cloak-pin above.

With creaking joints he knelt before Archbishop Green-field, and had to be assisted to rise. His Grace viewed the swaying figure with consternation, bade him be seated and then gave his attention to the parchment.

'Yes, a worthy document, Sir Robert. It would certainly carry great weight.'

He looked up to find that Robert's eyes were closed but that a smile of heavenly bliss had settled about his mouth. Poor young man! How to tell him that, in the end, his efforts were in vain?

'Sir Robert,' His Grace called gently, 'just one question, please: why did you do this? You are not connected with the family in any way.'

Robert opened his honest grey eyes.

'Because I love her,' he said.

The Archbishop sighed deeply: it was as he had feared.

'I have news for you, my son. She will be fully pardoned—'

The knight tried to bound off his bench, groaned and sank back.

'I thank Your Grace from my heart. May I be permitted to carry these tidings to her at Whorlton Castle?'

His Grace made patterns on the dusty floor with the toe of his shoe.

'She is no longer at Whorlton, my son. She has entered the Cistercian Order at Baysdale.'

THE NUNS AROSE at two o'clock in the morning, winter and summer, to sing Matins and Lauds. Their first Mass was celebrated at a quarter to five, then they recited Prime and the Martyrology in the Chapter Room.

Afterwards, Susanna read part of St. Benedict's Rule aloud and explained it tersely. On certain days this was followed by a Chapter of Faults and Accusations, each nun accusing herself of faults against the Rule, or pointing out, charitably, the shortcomings of others.

Then there was breakfast, which they called 'Mixt', followed by spiritual reading, study or a walk in the garden. At this time, a sister was permitted to address her superiors if she wished, before Tierce and the Conventual Mass at eight o'clock.

Now the manual labours of the day began and went on until late afternoon, interrupted only by Divine Office, mental prayer and the midday meal.

A small collation was eaten soon after five o'clock and, within two hours, the strains of the Salve Regina brought the Cistercian day to a close.

This was the time when Lucia's real torment began: she could not sleep at seven o'clock in the evening. Her thoughts wandered constantly to Whorlton, where light and music and conversation and company continued until midnight or later.

At last she would fall into an uneasy doze, to be awakened almost at once by the nuns' voices singing Matins.

During these first few weeks at Baysdale, it was Susanna's company which kept her sane. It was Susanna who advised that she lead her own life, as far as possible, without taking on the intolerable Cistercian burden. But, gradually, the routine of the household absorbed her. She began to attend the Conventual Mass. She abstained from meat. She learned to live for long periods in silence, and she began to work with her hands for the first time in her life, sewing, weaving, tending the garden. It was not that she liked doing any of these things; neither was she a prisoner within the building, but, slowly, the need for communion with these other women drove her to accept their ways.

It was only in the quiet of her cell at nights that she actually suffered, longing for her son, for her lover, for red meat and rough voices, for the sensuous, clinging satin of the dresses she had left behind at Whorlton, for freedom to ride away from Baysdale without being stared at, whispered about, even spat at in every village.

There was safety within the community. They called her simply 'my Lady', for Susanna had asked them to use her full name as little as possible, especially when traders or villagers were near, in order to save her from embarrassment. And as 'my Lady' she emerged an entirely new personality. The transformation took place slowly, over a period of almost three years...

13

In the year 1312, Edward II visited his northern provinces and announced that he would stay as guest of Nicholas de Menyll at Whorlton Castle. Nicholas at once sent a pressing invitation to Lucia at Baysdale, begging her to break her retreat and join the festivities, admitting candidly that he needed a woman of her ability to handle the royal occasion for him.

Now Nicholas had been generous to the little community at Baysdale during the three years of Lucia's sojourn there. Wagons had made frequent trips, loaded with wool and foodstuffs, and the artisans of Whorlton had repaired the buildings, and also erected a small new wing for Lucia's comfort and privacy. Sometimes, too, during the summer months, the young nurse Christina had been sent out to Baysdale with Whorlton's heir riding beside her. For this more than anything else, Lucia was grateful to Nicholas.

Now Susanna, the Abbess, was advising her to accept his invitation.

'It would be ungracious, at the least, to refuse him, Lucia. I ask you, for my sake, to go to Whorlton.'

But it was now as great an effort for Lucia to leave Baysdale as it had once been for her to stay in it. Here she had acquired the most impregnable form of virginity – that which comes to a mature woman after she has tasted, and laid aside, the pleasures of the world. Lucia had no curiosity left. The idea never crossed her mind, as it had in earlier days, that she was missing something. She had learned to blush again at a rough word. She had lost all appetite for meat and wine and had acquired a spiritual attitude of mind which Whorlton would surely offend.

Susanna folded her hands inside the huge sleeves of her cowl.

'Well?' she demanded tartly. 'Are you going to allow our gracious King to stay in a castle unblessed by woman's hand these three years'

'For the King,' Lucia said gently, 'I will go…'

SHE FOUND Whorlton in a state of unparalleled uproar and spent a frenzied week having linen prepared, silver polished, floors recovered, in between joyous bouts of games and riding with her five-year-old son and long, friendly discussions with Nicholas. But this latter relationship had altered profoundly. He had no physical interest whatsoever for her now, and he, in turn, was awed by her cheerful spirituality. He treated her with great deference and made no advances.

The day of the royal visit dawned and Lucia remembered with a tightening of the throat another day of similar excitement. In Kilton. For the games…

Guests arrived every hour. There was last-minute hammering and sawing. There were desperate pleas that she come quickly to various parts of the castle to see this and that. There was a bouncing five-year-old to be controlled, for poor Christina was in hysterics at the idea of beholding the King. Finally, Lucia threw up her hands and announced firmly that she was retiring to rest and dress.

As twilight gathered, the trumpets were heard in the distance and a procession of torch-bearers went out from the castle to lead in the King and his party.

Lucia, watching privately from the window of her own apartment, saw Edward the King ride into the courtyard. His corn-gold hair was reddened by the flare of the torches, his splendid shoulders were draped in a cloak of deep blue velvet, and his handsome face was wreathed in smiles. In spite of the distance and the crowd which separated them, she could feel the impact of his personality like a powerful heartbeat. It was one of the most unforgettable moments of her life when she saw Nicholas presenting their son to the King, and saw the King's hand rest briefly on the boy's head.

The banquet lasted far into the night. Lucia, who could eat little, feasted her eyes instead and stored up every sound and image of this great occasion. The King had an infectious humour and he laughed and mimicked and said outrageous things; he was the happiest, most carefree person in the Hall, to all outward appearances. Had he not just affixed he Great Seal to letters annulling Gaveston's exile? Soon his friend would be with him again. All would be well.

Now Alice the Red-haired sang a politically pointed ditty which convulsed the company with mirth and, although Edward laughed with the rest, it was doubtful if he fully understood the broad dialect and broader implications of the song. Jugglers juggled and musicians played.

At last, grown accustomed to the royal presence at her

elbow, Lucia managed to tear her gaze away from him to look around the crowded tables.

'Nicholas,' she whispered, 'that knight down there with the King's bodyguard – the second from the left – who is he?'

Nicholas squinted against the glare and smoke of the lights.

'Oh, a younger brother of Sir Adam Fitz-Robert de Everingham. They have connections in Laxton. I think this one is called Robert. Why?'

'I met him once…'

The knight looked up, feeling her eyes upon him. He smiled at her hesitantly. Even through the smoke, the clarity of his gaze was undimmed and the warmth of his friendship reached her. She raised a hand in acknowledgement.

The King, who never missed any side-play going on around him, even when he appeared absorbed in something else, now turned to Lucia and enquired casually:

'Did I understand you to say, fair lady, that you only met Sir Robert de Everingham once?'

'That is so, Sire. Briefly. At my aunt's funeral.'

'Then you must have made a profound impression upon him.' The Plantagenet eyes were bright with suspicion.

'I do not understand—'

'Have you forgotten the document that went to York when you were in some – er – difficulty with the Church?'

She replied, slowly:

'I knew of no document.'

'Tch, tch!' Edward said. 'How like our crusading knight to be so modest and retiring. Madam, be it known to you that Sir Robert de Everingham wore himself to a shade on your behalf. He was so ill with disappointment and grief when you shut yourself away in Baysdale that we had to wait six months for his recovery before claiming his services! Did you seriously believe that the good Greenfield of York quashed the proceedings against you purely out of the charity of his heart? Indeed no. A list of landowners' signatures on a petition, collected by de Everingham, was the instrument of your acquittal...'

She believed the King to be indulging in one of his more uncomfortable jests until she turned quickly to look at Nicholas. Then she knew that the truth had been spoken, and that Nicholas had never wanted her to hear it.

'I will thank Sir Robert personally and sincerely,' she said.

After the guests had arisen from the banqueting tables, she sent a page to summon de Everingham to a private room, and there she questioned him closely about his part in her acquittal.

'My lady,' he protested, 'it was your uncle, Sir Marmaduke, who set the petition in motion. His was the first signature and it was he who provided me with introductions to all the great houses in Cleveland, for I had been away many years and was a stranger and a foreigner in Cleveland. Also' – he smiled without bitterness – 'a younger brother, of no consequence.'

'But why did you interest yourself in my troubles?'

'Because I could not forget you after our meeting in the Priory.'

'Did you forget me afterwards, until tonight?'

'No.'

'Did you think me lost in Baysdale, then?'

'Lost to me. My lady, I beg of you to tell me, is it your intention to return there?'

'Would I be any less lost if I remained here at Whorlton?'

'You would be infinitely more so.'

She walked over to the unshuttered window and stood looking up at the night sky.

'I leave here in two days' time,' she said in a low voice. 'If my son were to remain, I doubt if I could tear myself away. But he is to be sent south to begin his remote preparation for knighthood. A mother has no say in the education of her sons: all mothers are accursed in their male children. It tears my heart to see a child of five summers sent to live among strangers.' Her throat contracted painfully and she stood silent, thinking of the long farewell, and then of the barren years stretching out before her. God, if only she could grasp life again, just once, and feel the pulse of creation in her...

'Sir Robert – I beg a favour of you, who have already done so much.'

He moved a step closer to her.

'It is that you will visit me occasionally at Baysdale. Tell me about the world. Let me warm my hands at the fire of other people's doings.'

He regarded her with compassion.

'Why must you shut yourself away again, my lady? If it is for penance, you have already done too much. You are young and beautiful and, to my eyes, virginal. If you return to Baysdale, my quest will end as before, when I knocked on the gates and was sent away like a small boy.'

She spun around in astonishment.

'You came to Baysdale?'

'Twice,' he said, his lips twitching into a smile. 'On both occasions, a tall, thin woman of icy aspect reduced me to a state of terror which no enemy charge could have done. She bade me ride away and return no more, saying that the Lady Lucia de Thweng wished for no visitors.'

Now Lucia began to giggle uncontrollably. Mirth over-rode her anger at Susanna's highhandedness.

'Anything,' she gasped, dabbing her eyes, 'anything would I have given to behold you and Susanna enraged in verbal combat! Oh, I must speak to her on my return. Never fear, Sir Robert, next time you will be admitted!'

AND SO HE WAS. During all that spring, while the King was in the North, Robert found many opportunities of visiting Baysdale, and sometimes he and Lucia would ride out together over the moors, with Christina – whom Lucia had brought with her from Whorlton, since she was no longer needed there after the heir's departure – following discreetly at a greater and greater distance.

But, as matters worsened for the King's cause, Robert's visits became hurried, infrequent, and finally ceased altogether. The colour drained from Lucia's life. Without Robert, there was no laughter, no interest: she was in love with him.

News of Gaveston's excommunication by Archbishop Winchelsea reached Baysdale, closely followed by tidings of the royal party's desperate evacuation of Newcastle: harried by Lancaster – whom Gaveston had nicknamed 'the fiddler' for some inscrutable reason – they left horse, treasure and arms behind and embarked for Scarborough, where the castle was strongly fortified on its forbidding hill above the North Sea.

For days and nights, Lucia lived in spirit with Robert de Everingham behind the grim walls of the fortress. She prayed incessantly for his safety and begged God to restore him to her, and her prayer was answered dramatically by the appearance of the copper-haired knight at Baysdale's gate.

'Lucia,' he said, when she ran to him, 'I have but a moment. We are trying to raise further troops. I must not delay—'

'Is Scarborough still in royal hands?'

'Gaveston is there, but Edward has ridden forth for help. Lucia, let us not talk of battles for this brief time. I have come many miles to see you. Our separation has grieved me bitterly.'

'It has grieved me also, Robert,' she said, 'but I have kept you in my heart and prayed God that you would return to me safely. I give thanks for sight of you whole and well!'

Her voice trembled and she turned her face away from his scrutiny.

'Lucia,' he said, 'Lucia, when it is over, will you be my lady and my wife?'

She had known that he would ask her sometime and she had decided to refuse: he was a man full of ideals, a virtuous – but not a pious – man: her life had made her unworthy of him and she loved him too much to wish such a woman as herself upon him. It was love which had taught her this humility. But now, the proposal, coming suddenly after the shock of his arrival, scattered all her preconceptions and, when she answered, it was from her heart.

'I would sooner die than live apart from you.'

They touched hands briefly, knowing that eyes were upon them from garden and pasture and building. Then he mounted his horse, smiled down at her with a new proprietary air, and rode quickly away.

THE TROOPS which Edward and his officers managed to raise were of little avail. During their absence from Scarborough Castle, the wily Lancaster called upon Piers Gaveston to surrender, telling him that his King's return had been delayed and that the men left to guard him would starve. Piers, foolish to the last, believed Lancaster and agreed to surrender the castle upon a solemn promise that his own life should be spared.

Under escort, the favourite was taken to Deddington Rectory in Oxfordshire and there held in uneasy custody by Pembroke and Henry Percy, both of whom knew that the baronial meeting at St. Paul's, earlier in the year, had agreed to Gaveston's death. But it was the manner of this death which troubled these two: they – and Lancaster also – wanted him fairly tried, found guilty of many crimes – and publicly executed with the King's consent.

The Earl of Warwick, however, whom Gaveston had always called 'the Black Dog', had other ideas. His hatred of the favourite was fanatical, and now he lay in wait, with his men, outside Deddington Rectory, in the darkness and the mud.

Warwick was a shrewd man and he knew that Pembroke was a bored one. Not far away, at Bampton, was Pembroke's wife. The chances were that Pembroke would go to visit her. This he did, leaving Henry Percy sleeping peacefully by the fire.

Now Warwick struck. He hauled Gaveston out of bed by the hair, hurled his crumpled clothing at him and ordered him to dress at sword point.

'W-when the K-King hears of this,' Gaveston stuttered, 'he will have your head.'

Alas, it was Piers' handsome head which rolled. After a hasty, secret trial in Warwick Castle, he was executed on

Blacklow Hill a mile outside the town of Warwick, on the nineteenth day of June in the year 1312.

The comment of the King, when news of his friend's death was brought to him, masked a depth of misery within himself.

'By God,' he said, 'what a fool he was! I could have told him never to get into Warwick's hands…'

Then Edward betook himself to the country and spent three weeks digging a most unnecessary ditch. He did not rest from his labours even to attend Mass on Sundays; for which, of course, he was criticised.

But the King's grief for his friend's murder was very real, and from the day of the execution onward he cherished a bitterness, a malice and a hatred for anyone who crossed him, which altered his once sunny disposition to a snarling sullenness.

The last act which Edward performed for the man he had loved was to remove his body from Oxford to King's Langley. And again there was a public outcry.

14

R obert and Lucia were married in the tiny chapel at Baysdale one spring morning in the year 1313. The chaplain performed the ceremony and the nuns sang the Mass which followed.

Susanna wept, kissed Robert and Lucia on each cheek, led them to a simple meal, and afterwards waved them farewell as they rode away to their new life in the manor house of Brotton, which was part of Lucia's estate. Christina was to follow them after a few days.

Now Lucia grasped her happiness firmly and showed herself to be such an excellent wife that everyone marvelled – everyone except Robert, who had known that she was without fault from the start! He revelled in her affection like a small boy being spoilt and enjoying it. Whenever she threatened to postpone a promised treat for them both, he would plead:

'No, Lucia, not tomorrow. Today. Let us live *now*. Let us be fully conscious of every pleasant and beautiful thing.'

With him, it was the knowledge that soon he would be recalled to battle; with her, the instinct to store against the empty future when he would be gone. They were both aware that the long honeymoon days at Brotton could not continue indefinitely in a land so troubled.

She hoped that she might be with child by him before he left her, but, as the loving weeks wore on and she did not become pregnant, she regarded it as an omen: this love was to be a brief, brilliant interlude in her life. It was to end without trace. She always knew that.

The harvest of that year was a bad one throughout the country and, in the North, a series of Scottish raids had done untold damage to every living thing on the land. The people faced a bleak winter and, at first, blamed the Scots entirely for it.

For Edward the King, this bad harvest was the beginning of the end. As always, people were more concerned about the price of bread than about the national policy which determined it. If it were the Scots who had ruined the land, then it was Edward's fault for not subduing the Scots. If, on the other hand, the entire visitation was a result of the wrath of God, then it was the King's wickedness which had brought this upon the country. Either way, Edward could not escape blame. Fortunately for him, however, nobody was given a glimpse of the future: six years of famine stalking the land; crops poisoned by weeds, cattle dying from eating the poison; fowl-pest in the poultry runs; foot-rot among the flocks; black blight on the fruit crops...

For the time being, it was decided to concentrate on the Scots as the greatest enemy. A series of punitive expeditions went forth, all building up to the King's massive defeat at Bannockburn in 1314.

From this massacre Robert returned safely to Brotton, but Lucia's first husband, William le Latimer, was taken prisoner by the Bruce. She was too much relieved by the former circumstance to exult over the latter one.

Now the country was firmly in the grip of famine, but Lucia schemed for Robert's comfort and they spent one winter together in memorable happiness, doing their best by their tenants and helping the widows and orphans of men killed at Bannockburn.

During these months, doors opened to Lucia which had been shut in her face many years previously. As the devoted wife of a good and honest man she was accepted by all, and many new friendships enriched her life. She bore no grudges against those who had once spurned her.

Lucia was to remember that winter all her life, for it was the last one that she and Robert spent together. Before the snows thawed he was sent again to Scotland, and was killed there the following year, without having returned home in the meanwhile.

Through the February mud, she had his body carried to Guisborough and buried in the Priory beside Isabel's, on the spot where they had first met. Then she returned to Brotton, gathered the orphan children once more about her table and went on with the work which had to be done in starving Cleveland.

Her hair was greying now – she was thirty-seven – and she gave no further thought to her appearance, but went with her skirts looped up high over her girdle as the nuns used to do when they worked on the land, and her unbuttoned sleeves rolled above her elbows in defiance of all convention.

By nightfall she had worked herself into a state of exhaustion that she slept, unweeping. Each day she cared for the children in increasing numbers and visited widows and old people, bringing them smaller and smaller quantities of food from Brotton's emptying cellars.

Often, it seemed to her, Robert walked by her side. She saw the colour of his hair in summer beech leaves, heard his voice in the wind, urging her on when she was too weary to move.

'No, Lucia, not tomorrow. Today...'

The memory of him comforted her spirit, but her body cried out for his body. Yet only in death could she hope to lie beside him once again.

Two YEARS of unremitting labour passed. Had she not seen the nuns of Baysdale work like serfs, Lucia would not have believed that any woman, least of all herself, could work as she did now. Undernourished and overtired, she took to her bed for a few days, troubled by the pain in her chest which she had suffered years previously. She employed this respite by taking stock of her estate and of her scattered family. The legal tangles resulting from Robert's death were now finally cleared up, and she could review her position in its entirety.

Her son by Nicholas de Menyll was now recognised as heir of Whorlton. Her other son, William le Latimer, was acting Lord of Danby for his father, who was now a Commander in the King's army, having been released by the Bruce the previous year. The Inquisition following Robert de Everingham's death found that Lucia and her late husband had been enfeoffed of the manors of Brotton and Kirkburn; of ten marcs' rent in Skin-ningrove; and of half the Bailiwick of Langbargh in special tail – with remainder to Robert's heirs – and of the manor of Yarm, with remainder to young Nicholas de Menyll.

Robert, himself a younger brother, had no property of

his own to leave, and his sole heir was found to be a nephew, Adam Fitz-Adam de Everingham of Laxton.

Thus the marriage ended as though it had never been, except for the consolidation of the change in Lucia's character, begun at Baysdale. Nobody spoke of her now as the 'Helen of Cleveland'. After six years of toil and famine her beauty was almost entirely gone. Only those who could see summer's splendour in a winter's tree, or admire the tree as it stood, bare and stark, every year of its age etched upon it, would now give Lucia de Everingham a second glance.

She was the Lady of Brotton, a worthy woman, loved by dozens of children, respected by men and women. But she lived alone except for her retainers.

She was fond of her manor house at Brotton and had long since decided to spend the remainder of her days there. Situated amid the countryside which she knew intimately from childhood, and only a short ride from Kilton Castle, its solar window framed one of the loveliest views in Cleveland. Here she would sit, looking across at the North Sea and along the jagged coastline from the Tees' mouth to the Coatham salt marshes. In the summer-time the north-westerly light poured in through the high, narrow window. She had two window-seats made in oak, covered with red velvet bankers.

The spring of 1320 presaged the end of the famine, and by June healthy crops were high and fruit already ripening. Tenants' children, no longer hungry, came less often now, but she could see them out in the fields and lanes, still resplendent in the clothing she had had made for them out of her personal wardrobe.

Her own apparel was simple these days. She wore the dull, modest dresses which had served her at Baysdale and, on her head, a wimple and coif of white linen. The dresses hung loose upon her; she was very thin.

Now it was the solar which occupied her attention almost completely. This was her refuge from the noise and tumult of the Hall, and she retired to it more and more. There was a wall fireplace which smoked less than the central brazier type; a petch for hanging clothes; some heavy oak chests and benches; a prie-dieu and a carved chair. The walls were oak-panelled to a height of four feet and the ceiling was rounded above beams. Onto this bare background, Lucia had grafted a good deal of comfort. She had hung skins and tapestries above the panelling, and had preserved Robert's sword and hunting knives and armour by way of ornament. Recently she had bought a small, oriental carpet from a travelling merchant, and had the trefoil above the window glazed in red. These things pleased her enormously. Now there was a brocade curtain in process of being made to replace the leather one which separated her bedchamber from the solar.

She was a wealthy woman indulging her tastes, drawing warmth and security about her to shut out loneliness, boredom, stagnation. She was forty-one years of age, at peace with God and her neighbour but not always with herself. The old restlessness persisted, to travel, to meet people, even to love again... How absurd that latter seemed, how remote. By the standards of her day, she was practically an old woman. To dream of men and children at this age was, for a widow, almost immoral.

But Lucia, on her window-seat, embroidering a bonnet for her cousin Margaret's new baby, dreamed of love and smiled with her eyes.

'Only the body grows old,' she said aloud. 'The mind and the heart reach maturity and age no further after that.'

Her steward, John Peacock, passed under the window, and she leaned out and called to him.

'John, come up to the solar, will you? How is Christina?'

Christina had married Lucia's steward the previous year and, the day before yesterday, had given birth to twins.

John Peacock entered the solar, carefully avoiding the carpet with his mud-caked felt shoes.

'John,' Lucia said, after the twins and their mother had been discussed, 'I am very pleased with the red glass in the trefoil, but now I hear that clear glass is being made in Venice, and I shall not rest until the entire window is filled in. Where can I find a merchant who will undertake the work of measuring and shipping?'

Her steward looked at her aghast.

'It would cost a king's ransom,' he said, 'even if it could be done — which I doubt. There is only one man who would undertake such a thing.'

'Who is that?' she asked eagerly, but John Peacock shook his head.

'I know not his name. He owns a ship called the *Gaillard*. Anchors at Whitby, maybe once every three of four years. He's a Frenchman but comes from Venice, they say.'

'And he trades in glass?'

'No, no, lady, he doesn't trade. He's a soldier, I think. Has a company of archers on board to guard the treasures the *Gaillard* carries. He chooses rare and costly things, sometimes for himself, sometimes for anyone who asks him, and ships them all over the world from as far away as Byzantium. They say it's his pastime when he's not soldiering for the Doge.'

'You're very well informed, John,' Lucia smiled. 'How is that?'

He shuffled his feet.

'I took ale many a time with his archers, lady.'

'I see. What a curious man he sounds. When was he in Whitby Harbour last?'

John Peacock considered.

'It was just before Sir Robert was killed, lady. A long time now…'

'Yes. Well, keep your ears open in the alehouses, John. Let me know when the *Gaillard* is seen again.'

She decided that John had made most of the story up to please her, and forgot about it at once. Therefore she was much surprised when her steward came to see her about the same matter less than three months later.

'The *Gaillard* has been stood off Whitby for two nights now. There's a heavy sea still running, but boats are going out to help her in today!'

THE SEPTEMBER MORNING was jewel-bright and the wind had dropped since sunrise. Lucia and John Peacock set out from Brotton. They reached Whitby as the Abbey bells were ringing the midday angelus, and made their way on foot along the crowded quayside, Lucia picking her steps among scattered fish and wet nets, while her steward walked ahead brandishing a large stick and growling at small boys who, in turn, stared at the lady.

The *Gaillard* was moored in the deeper water at the end of the quay. She was a graceful ship, not over-cluttered with defences. She seemed to be in the sole charge of a barefooted old man whom John Peacock addressed.

'He says the master is below,' John told Lucia, as she reached him.

The old man shouted something and a voice called back from the depths:

'A lady. I'm coming up.'

She saw the speaker's hands first, very thin and brown: then the top of his head – fairish hair cut short all around.

Blinking, he came up into the sunlight, a slightly-built man in a short, rough, grey tunic and blue chausses.

He looked up at her, stopped dead and said:

'Lucia!'

Confused, she stared at him, trying to remember who he was. Then he smiled, bowed and said:

'Bartholomew de Fanacourt, at your service, my lady!'

'Bartholomew…' The little page with whom she had run away from Kirkburn over twenty years before.

John Peacock, grinning, melted away and dragged the bare-footed old man with him. Lucia and Bartholomew began to talk, and it was a conversation that went on, with few interruptions, for the rest of the day. The *Gaillard* needed repairs after her buffeting in the September gales, so her master set his crew of archer-sailors free and left the craftsmen of Whitby to work on the ship. He himself rode to Brotton with Lucia.

'How long,' she wanted to know, 'did it take you to reach home after you left me at Kilton?'

'Five years,' he replied solemnly.

'Five *years*?'

'Aye. I reached the Port of London and was taken aboard by a wool-master sailing for Venice. He said he would set me down in France on the return journey, but he died on reaching home. Venice was conducting one of her many wars when I arrived, so I enlisted under the Doge's standard and was shipped to Africa instead!'

'But you did go home, eventually?'

'Oh, yes. All was changed, though, and I had fallen in love with Venice – with her independence and her way of forging ahead, with the beauty of everything about her, with her free spirit. I had to return.'

'Why, then, do you leave her to come to these northern waters?'

The September twilight was drawing in and she could not see his face clearly as he rode beside her.

'To look for you,' he said.

She laughed gently.

'A likely tale! I think you are a professional lover…'

He sighed patiently, and reached into a pocket in his cloak lining.

'I shall prove it to you.'

He handed her a flat leather case and their horses moved close together – as on the moor, long ago.

She slid her fingertips over the surface and felt the rounded outlines of the three popinjays.

'It is twenty years old,' he said, 'but every time I came to look for you, it was either too late – or too early.'

She knew what he meant – his last visit had been but a few months before she was widowed – but curiosity about the other visits made her ask:

'What do you mean?'

'I heard from a knight in Rome that you had returned to le Latimer after four years at Kilton. "This," said I to myself, "cannot last." So, I bought the *Gaillard* and sailed for the first time into Whitby, where I intended to make discreet enquiry for you. But the town was buzzing with Sheriff's orders and the like, and I discovered that my love was at Mulgrave Castle, making merry with de Mauley. So I sailed away again.'

She thought sadly:

If only you had come for me then, how different my life might have been… But, no: she did not regret any part of it. It was best left alone.

Aloud she asked:

'And your second visit, when was that?'

'Three years later. You had just borne an heir for Whorlton.'

She asked without anger:

'Are you deliberately taunting me with my past?'

'On the contrary, I am using it to prove that your doubt of me is unfounded. When I visited Cleveland again, behold, you were in a nunnery! Now, if I were a professional lover, I would have laid siege to the place, or scaled the walls at least. But I have adopted a republic as my country, and therefore I respect the right of everyone to please themselves, in so far as they can, without interference from others. You had made a series of choices – none of them involving me – and I had not the impertinence to question them.'

'So now you come,' she said, 'and find an old woman.'

'An old woman?' he asked, out of the darkness. 'Do you see me then as an old man? In truth, we are of almost equal age.'

'You do not seem like an old man to me,' she laughed.

The lights of Brotton Manor winked through the trees and they went in together to the evening meal.

Sir Bartholomew sat beside Lucia at the High Table; there were no other guests. But the retainers, eating off their platters at the side tables, noted how animatedly she talked and how intently she listened to this weather-browned man whose fair hair was bleached almost white in front by wind and salt spray. They noted how much she laughed and how long she dallied over the meal. When she and the master of the *Gaillard* went into the solar together afterwards, a knowing wink travelled right round the Hall.

'Now, open the leather case,' Bartholomew said.

She untied the thongs and opened it out. Inside were five compartments.

'There are five gifts,' he said, 'each for a different age of your life.'

He stood behind her as she lifted each one out.

The first was a single pearl, flawless, exquisite, gold-mounted on a hair-fine chain.

'A gift for a young girl,' he said.

The second was a tiny mirror – the first she had ever seen in glass – enclosed in a frame of silver filigree.

'A gift for a beautiful young woman.'

The third was a phial of rose essence.

'A gift for a great lady.'

The fourth, a pair of gloves of such fine leather that they could almost be pushed into a thimble.

'For a woman who had hidden herself away from the world, a sign of friendship.'

And the fifth was a beautiful gold mesh snood with a single emerald trembling over the brow, like clear water in a green-shaded place.

'For a widow who believes herself old because a few silver ribs shine in her hair.'

She had no words to thank him. The gifts alone were perfect in themselves, but the fact that they had been collected for her over twenty years touched and moved her as nothing else in her life had ever done.

'If only I had known of such remembrance,' she said without turning.

But he replied:

'You did know, only would not believe. That night in the hut on the moors, I told you that I would never forget you. You answered me that there were many women in the world. Very well. I have taken a goodly number to my bed, but not one of them could release me from my promise to you, although it has meant nothing to you – until now.'

'Why now?'

'Because now you are lonely and uncherished, two things which mark a woman's face more than age or hardship. Lucia, I am a wandering foreigner. If you cannot love me for myself, will you take me for my faithfulness?'

'You mean – *marriage*? Now, at my age?' She was thunderstruck.

He made a gesture of impatience, caught her by the shoulders and swung her around to face him.

'You are forty-one,' he said brutally. 'What do you intend to do with the next thirty years or so of your life?'

'I – I had decided to settle here, quietly…'

'Quietly, Lucia? Oh, be truthful: you are bored already. Come and let me show you the busy, noisy world. In Venice you can have your hair dyed red. In Flanders you can choose the cloth for dresses to be sewn in Italy. They will make you shoes in Cordova to dance in London. Lucia, you *must* want these things!'

She began to laugh.

'All I really wanted this morning,' she said, 'was glass for that window. Now – well, I've always envied Catherine, my cousin's wife, her lovely red hair.'

'You'll come to Venice? Lucia, I have loved you for twenty years. There would be no indecent haste if we went tonight! I have a tall white house there, its feet in the sea. There is a view of St. Mark's from the upper windows. Lucia, you'll come? As my wife?'

She felt dizzy and more than a little mad. She remembered that widows often made disastrous marriages and that foreigners were untrustworthy, that ships were wrecked every day, or set upon by enemies, and that Venice had frequent epidemics.

'Yes,' she said.

15

Lucia required that there should be no uproar concerning her forthcoming marriage to Bartholomew. She had lived quietly for too long and had no wish to reawaken old echoes. Bartholomew understood this very well.

They sat on the red velvet bankers by the tall window and looked out at the star-shimmering sea.

'What is the latest we can leave for Venice?' she asked.

'It would be well to cross the Channel before November, Lucia. But you will have much preparation...'

'Yes. I shall tell John Peacock and his wife, Christina, without delay. They can move into my apartments here: the stewardship will come easier that way and the rooms will not look forlorn when we return. We *will* return, Bartholomew?'

All at once she was afraid of leaving Cleveland and the familiar things she had gathered about her, for a strange home in a strange land. Her need to be with Bartholomew was overwhelming; it had come upon her with the sudden-ness of a mountain torrent, the desire to look at him, to touch him, but she realised that there was much about him which she did not know and might never know.

He reached out in the darkness and took her hand. Even this small contact gave her infinite pleasure, and she closed her eyes, savouring it.

'We will return in the spring if you wish it, my love,' he said. 'If you have not enjoyed your winter in Venice, we will then remain here in Cleveland.'

It was impossible to worry about anything for long when Bartholomew was by her side. He had a knack of smoothing all difficulties, of inspiring confidence. Her only real fear was that she might fail to please him. With all her heart, she wished that her body were ten years younger for him to enjoy her more.

'Tomorrow,' she said briskly, 'we will ride over to Kilton to tell my cousin, William, and his wife, of our plans. Apart from my Uncle Marmaduke, there is no one else need know.'

This desire for privacy on her part was an unwillingness to share him with anybody. During the few days of his stay at Brotton she had been impatient of any intrusion into their company. Yet she recognised that he was a man who liked and needed people about him.

'If I am not more careful,' she told herself seriously, 'I will drive him away.' And the idea filled her with terror.

She had not visited Kilton often of late, fearing her company too dull for the guests who assembled there these last years. Rumour had it that William was a dissolute baron, engaged in all manner of devilries, egged on by the childless and discontented Catherine, but to Lucia the present master and mistress of Kilton were still children, incapable of crime. They always welcomed her warmly and she was grateful to them for that. They even vacated the popinjay bed when she wished to stay the night!

The day on which she and Bartholomew rode to Kilton was clear and warm with all the heavy beauty of September. They rode slowly through the berried woods, talking, reminiscing, laughing together as though their friendship of twenty years previously had never been suspended. Bartholomew's greatest gift with Lucia was that he could always make her laugh; he had a turn of phrase, a grimace, an expressive gesture with his hard, thin hands which found instant response in her.

The castle gates were open and people moved in and out, carrying wood and foodstuffs, driving animals, riding mules and ponies, shouting, gossiping, bargaining as though the Wards were a market square. A blind beggar prayed aloud for all sinners as he knelt in the dust, and three children were playing at how near they could approach him without his knowing. The red-headed cross-eyed lad who used to tend Lucia's horse in the old days was now a wizened old man, although not forty years old; he still tended horse at Kilton's gate.

'Go, tell the Lady Catherine I am here,' Lucia ordered him now, 'with Sir Bartholomew de Fanacourt.'

They proceeded at leisure towards the Inner Ward and, presently, Catherine came flying to meet them.

'Lucia, it is a lifetime since you came! Who—?'

'Catherine, this is Sir Bartholomew de Fanacourt from the Republic of Venice. We want to talk to you and William, if that is convenient.'

Lucia looked away quickly from Catherine's face. The sunlight was very strong and, for an instant, had been unkind to the red-haired woman, showing the fine lines that spread like a spider's web around eyes and nose and mouth. Was she who had blossomed as an exquisite flower to shrivel up like a mouldering nut because she had not fulfilled the purpose of womanhood? The idea filled Lucia with sadness, for she was fond of Catherine and had often stood speechless before her beauty.

William joined them for the morning meal – he was not long out of bed and his eyelids were alarmingly swollen – and Lucia told him and Catherine the news of her forth-coming marriage.

'No one else must know,' she added quietly, looking at Bartholomew.

'Nonsense,' William shouted, suddenly awake. 'We must have a banquet. Invite everybody. It's been weeks since this table was fully laid. You must be married here in St. Peter's.'

'William, *please*, not—'

'Of course, Lucia,' Catherine piped. 'We welcome any excuse for a celebration. Do not deny us!'

It was a sad little plea from a bored woman, although delivered with all the gaiety of former years.

'Very well,' Lucia said, after another glance at Bartholomew, who was laughing. 'You are very kind, both of you.'

William and Catherine made it a memorable wedding for the de Fanacourts. With characteristic abandon, they slaughtered every living thing in their winter game reserves to load the banqueting tables. They indulged in the supreme folly of burning all their stocked wood in early October to heat every room in the castle.

It was a wonderful feast and guests came from every part of Cleveland. Even Marmaduke, ageing and slow, made the journey from Thwing. Gifts piled up in the private apartments, and on St. Peter's Chapel Catherine lavished flowers and lace, wax and candles and scented tapers, until the little room looked like a corner of heaven's garden on a starry night.

Lucia had made only one request: that no more than a

dozen people should witness the ceremony. Therefore, when her priest-cousin, Thomas from Kirkleatham, pronounced her the wife of Sir Bartholomew de Fanacourt, there was no crowding of St. Peter's as during her first marriage, no jostling and neck-craning. There was only a great peace into which the words of the Liturgy dropped gently while the tapers and candles burned.

The *Gaillard* was waiting on the morning tide. Lucia embraced her cousins, Catherine and William, and all the friends who had made the dawn journey from Kilton to Whitby.

'Goodbye! Goodbye!'

Bartholomew handed her aboard and the archers stood to attention among the boxes and packages that littered the deck, containing Lucia's clothing and her wedding gifts. Bartholomew put his arm about her waist and held her tightly to him.

The shores of Cleveland began to slip away into the greyness as the *Gaillard* headed east in search of deep water and a strong wind before turning at last southward for the Channel, Biscay and the Mediterranean.

ON THE FIRST day of February, in 1321, there was snow on St. Mark's Square and yellow foam on the Grand Canal, although the sky overhead was a brilliant summer blue.

Lucia wanted to go on looking forever at the palaces and the people, the ships and the bridges. There were women wearing clogs. There were Jews with yellow patches on their chests. There were men whose tunics were trimmed with point coupé and air point lace. And everywhere there was bustle and trade and excitement.

But the big gondola with its striped awning, into which

she and Bartholomew had stepped from the *Gaillard*, moved into quieter waterways. Here and there was a glimpse of a muddy alley, with a horse or a mule walking slowly along. Further on, there was much trailing greenery and little trees.

The gondolier moored his craft to a black post in the water.

'We're home, Lucia,' Bartholomew said.

She looked up at the tall white house with its pillared doorway, its window-ledges green with shrubs and all its walls festooned with tumbling flowered creeper. Where water met stone, there was a deep border of moss.

'The house with its feet in the sea!' she breathed, and he laughed, delighted, and hugged her to him under the shade of the awning.

Servants flocked to the entrance of the house to welcome their master and, with delight and astonishment, their new mistress. Luggage was unloaded from the gondola. There was a scurrying to and fro – braziers full of glowing coals being carried to the upper rooms, bundles of clean, fresh linen, trays of food. It seemed that the whole house leapt to life as soon as Bartholomew stepped into it, and Venetian servants had a great capacity for laughter and chatter and song.

It was a bright, airy house, high-ceilinged. The sparkling water outside was reflected on the walls like leaping silver fishes, and everywhere was the smell of the sea.

Every room through which they walked was filled with exquisite furniture and ornaments, and in their bedchamber all the loveliness of Byzantium had been captured in cloth and metal and paint.

Bartholomew pulled her down on a couch beside him.

'Talk to me, Lucia.'

'I am smitten dumb with wonder!'

'Tell me if you like all you see.'

'Everything pleases here. How many women helped you to plan this room alone?'

'There is only one woman,' he said, bending over her, 'and I am going to love her now because, tomorrow, she will be too busy for me. As soon as it is known that I have brought a wife to Venice, she will be besieged by merchants and dressmakers, hair-dyers and scent-bottlers, goldsmiths, silversmiths and workers in leather. They will all flock here like hungry gulls. And my lady must be careful, for extrava-gance in colour and length of cloth is against the law here. One must not outshine the Dogessa!'

'Is that true, Bartholomew?' Lucia sat up.

'Certainly. Only last year a lady was arrested in the Square by one of the Savi for having too much cloth in her sleeves. Do not worry, my love. The laws are only made against bad taste.'

She lay back against his arm again, vaguely disquieted. She realised that the complicated structure of a great trading republic required more rules to uphold it than did the loosely-knit wilderness of Cleveland, but it was strange thinking that set such importance upon the width of a lady's sleeve.

'The making of petty rules and regulations spreads like a disease,' she said slowly.

Bartholomew kissed her shoulder.

'You must not worry about such things. I only mentioned the matter to spare you argument with dressmakers.'

'Nevertheless, I *do* worry.'

'Not now,' he said, kissing her. 'Not now…'

She was with child by him since before Christmas, and her breasts were large and firm. The famished, blue-veined look which she had had since Cleveland's famine years was gone; age had melted away from her with the smoothing of the lines in her face. She was happier, more carefree than she had ever been in her life.

Soon, the arts and fashions of Venice were to complete the transformation. On the day after her arrival she sat in the sunshine of the roof-top garden while a hairdresser and his assistant tinted her silvering locks a reddish gold. She viewed the results in a large mirror of Murano glass and was as pleased as a child with a new toy. Red-gold hair! Such a gift she had never dreamed of.

From the dressmakers she ordered gowns in Persian silk which conformed to the 'one-colour' rule of the Savi but were shot through with a thousand tints. She ordered Venetian lace gowns for the expected child.

She and Bartholomew visited the famous island of Murano, where the glass-blowers were an aristocracy and a law unto themselves, and her husband chose a wedding gift for her there: a set of a dozen goblets in glass finer than silk and with the fire and sparkle of diamonds. The stem of each goblet was fashioned like a stalk with leaves budding from it. Each vein in every leaf was traced with needle-fine precision as they supported the fragile, hollow flower, with fluted rim outlined in gold, which would contain the liquid. By contrast with the goblets there was a pair of slender jugs for wine and oil, smooth-bodied as young trees, and tall and narrow. It was a joy to look from the jugs to the goblets and back again.

This wonderful gift was packed, each piece separately, in silk and then in lambs' wool and then in straw before being encased in a carved wooden box. It was the expression of a rich man's love.

Lucia revelled in this love and in the importance of her husband in Venetian society. He was in constant demand as an adviser on artistic matters, and they both dined together at a different house or palace almost every night. When guests came to Bartholomew's residence, the Murano goblets were twirled between fine fingers and discussed and admired. Afterwards, Lucia washed them herself. They were too precious to her to be allowed into servants' hands.

Bartholomew was also a familiar figure among the ships in which Venice took such pride. His maps and drawings were greatly prized in the Arsenal, and he was allowed to wander freely in this gigantic shipyard which the Republic guarded as her greatest treasure.

There were few people, from Doge Giovanni Soranzo himself down to the poorest workman, who did not know the name of Bartholomew de Fanacourt, and Bartholomew himself collected friends with the same enthusiasm as he collected works of art and details of shipbuilding. Through him, Lucia became acquainted with the Golden Book nobility and also with the lively burghers and their talented wives, who wrote and painted and made music while the nobles yawned in boredom. Burghers' wives and children were the really free and independent citizens of Venice; Jews were tolerated but restricted; the nobility shackled its womenfolk and sent its children away to be educated at a very early age.

'I *like* the burghers,' Lucia announced with finality. 'They are creative. Let us never aspire to be noble here, Bartholomew. I will not have my child taken away from me, for the sake of fashion, when it is two or three years old.'

He put his hand over hers.

'But you would like its name in the Golden or Silver Book?'

'No, I think not, even if it could be arranged. We are foreigners here and Venice is a jealous power.'

He shook his head in bewilderment.

'Lucia, you say you love Venice and that you are happy here. Why then do you attribute the most sinister motives to every move of her officials?'

'It is something which I feel but do not understand,' she replied.

In that August, Lucia bore her husband a daughter whom they named Alicia, a child of great beauty and vitality who was to be a joy to her parents all their lives.

The curse of Kirkburn was broken at last.

16

While Lucia was still resting after the birth of her daughter, Bartholomew had a visitor from England whose arrival seemed to disturb him. He took the man up to the roof garden where they could speak privately.

'Now, Thornborrow, what did you want with me that you should greet me so strangely?'

'I merely told you, sir, that friends of the House of Lancaster will assemble in Whitby at the end of February.'

'What is that to me? An event almost seven months hence and many countries away.'

'The Earl said that you would come if I could find you. It will take until the spring to raise and train the necessary army.'

'But for what purpose? I know not what happens in England lately.'

Bartholomew was impatient to end this interview.

'I must speak with you,' Thornborrow said earnestly.

They sat on the parapet furthest away from the house.

'Tell me something important, then. I have little time to waste.'

'You know that Lancaster's wife was seduced by the Earl de Warenne with the King's approval?'

'Yes, yes. That happened five years ago—'

'The political situation of today arises out of that. The King and Lancaster now hate each other so bitterly that one or other must go.'

'But I heard that they exchanged the kiss of peace at Hathern.'

'They did. Things were better for a while. We had a two-year truce with Scotland and better harvests lowered the price of bread. Wheat came down from three shillings and fourpence to sixpence a bushel! The people were pleased.'

'What else happened? Go on, go on. All this I know.'

'Twenty-one carts came into York bearing the Doomsday Book and other records for the Courts of Justice to be held there.'

Bartholomew jumped up.

'I lose patience with you,' he said. 'I have only been a year out of England myself and all this happened before I left. Have you come so far to tell me so little?'

Thornborrow smiled.

'I merely wanted to know if you wished to hear more. Your impatience signifies that you do. Very well. There is a new favourite: the young Hugh Despenser – as clever as Gaveston was foolish. He is married to Eleanor of Clare, one of the three co-heiresses of the Earl of Gloucester.'

'Lancaster does not like this?'

'He does not. Nor do the Marcher earls, nor the Northern barons. The country is as near to civil war as makes no matter. The fear is that the Despensers could rule the land through Edward.'

'Why, then delay action until next April?'

'Because this last blow must be the final one. Whose aim is not true, dies.'

'And if Edward is killed?'

'We have an heir apparent. His son has been proclaimed Prince of Wales.'

'I see. Lancaster sent you to tell me all this?'

'Yes, to convince you that the position is desperate. He depends on you to join him.'

'What is my importance among so many of his loyal friends?'

Thornborrow shrugged.

'You know what has already happened between you and the Earl of Lancaster—'

'You must not mention that in this house.'

'Your wife does not know? I envy you not the explanation then. Her former husband and all her family were most loyal king's men...'

'Quiet. You overstep the bounds of your commission.'

Thornborrow, unperturbed, fell to studying the Venetian landscape spread out below him. There must be the islands of San Cristoforo and of Pace; the tall tower in the distance would be the Torcello, and that dark line along the water the forest of the island they called Deserto. To the left rose the Euganean Hills.

Bartholomew rubbed a hand across his forehead and surveyed the sweat upon his fingers. He cursed the promise he had made ten years previously to the King of England's greatest enemy.

'Thornborrow, tell the Earl that I will come to Whitby at the end of April with a full crew of trained archers.'

Bartholomew went down slowly to his wife's bedchamber.

'Who was your visitor, my love?' she asked.

'Eh? Oh – a man – about a cargo.'

'I thought his voice sounded English. Was it?'

'Possibly.'

'This heat does not agree with you, Bartholomew. You look tired. Lie down a little while. It is cool here with the shades drawn.'

'No,' he said, 'no…' and began to pace about the room, then suddenly changed his mind and went and lay down beside her.

'Lucia, you would like to go home for a little while, would you not? Home to Cleveland?'

She flushed with pleasure and excitement.

'Oh, Bartholomew, yes! Just for a time, of course. Do not think that I dislike Venice—'

'But you miss the long rides over the moors, eh? You miss your own people? You wish to show them your little daughter?'

'It would be nice to see Marmaduke again, and William and Catherine, and to make sure that everything is well at Brotton.'

'It is arranged then. In a few weeks you should be well and strong. We will spend the worst part of the winter in the Château de Fanacourt in the South of France; that should please you, for you have often wanted to see the estates there of which you are mistress. Then, in the spring, we will set out for England…'

'How long will we be away, Bartholomew?'

'Ah, it is difficult to say. It may even be a year or so.'

'Surely it could not take us a year or so to see to our estates in France and England? Our daughter is still very young for such a journey. When you first mentioned it, I had half-considered leaving her here with her nurse if we were to be away for no more than six months.'

'Cleveland produces fine women,' he smiled, kissing

her. 'I think a few seasons there will do our Alicia good. It is her heritage, Lucia.'

He hoped he had convinced her and that there was no suspicion in her mind that his motives were other than stated. He determined not to tell her the real reason for his visit to England until she and her infant daughter were safely installed in the Brotton manor house. There, Lucia would feel secure, and free to make her choice between loyalty to her King and loyalty to her husband. To force this choice upon her in a foreign land, where she was still a comparative stranger, would be unjust, according to Bartholomew's code. To expect her to share cramped quarters aboard the *Gaillard* on a long journey with a rebel and a traitor would be unthinkable.

It was better that she did not know the truth.

WINTER PASSED PLEASANTLY IN FRANCE, and Bartholomew kept his archers in training by organising hunts and trials of skill and sending them on long journeys through the wooded, hilly country. At the first sign of spring, he had the *Gaillard* overhauled and began to check provisions for the second stage of their voyage.

It had not escaped Lucia's notice that her husband was restless and tense. Her own wish was to stay longer in the lovely Château de Fanacourt, where the baby Alicia thrived, but she made no mention of this and pretended to be as anxious as Bartholomew was to see Dover. The pretence, however, was not necessary once the *Gaillard* began to edge her way up the east coast of England in the teeth of a February gale; Lucia was the happiest returning exile Cleveland had ever welcomed.

'Oh, Christina!' she gasped when they reached Brotton, 'it's good to be home.'

'Not as good as it is to have you home, my lady.' Christina plumped the red velvet bankers of the window-seats, straightened the bright wool rug by the fireplace, gave the dead Sir Robert's armour a polish with her sleeve. Then she took the seven-month-old baby in her arms and talked to her and sang and danced about the floor while Lucia laughed happily and Bartholomew watched them inscrutably.

'A little dark-haired girl,' Christina enthused, 'the image of my lady.' She shot Bartholomew an apologetic glance but his mind seemed to be a long way off.

'I'm glad she was a girl,' Lucia whispered. 'All my troubles lay in my sons and their fathers!'

Bartholomew saw the look which passed between the women, a look of friendship and shared memories and understanding, and he was glad he had brought Lucia home.

Now they were chattering about dresses and fashions in hair-styling; about Christina's twins; about John Peacock... He was glad when a servant brought wine and cheese, and Christina took her leave, carrying little Alicia out with her.

'Lucia,' he said unsmilingly, 'when we have eaten and rested a little, I must talk with you.'

She had never seen him look so grim. A little chill of apprehension touched her spine.

'Whatever it is, Bartholomew,' she said gently, 'has waited to be said since we left Venice.'

'You knew then?'

'Yes. And I knew that you would tell me in your own time. For some reason, you wanted to see me settled here in Brotton before you spoke.'

He stood in front of Sir Robert's armour and addressed himself to the empty helmet.

'This country, Lucia, is on the brink of civil war. One must take sides. Whom do you favour?'

Bartholomew was never abrupt in his speech but had rather learnt the Venetian habit of describing everything in detail and at length. She was too taken aback by his sudden brevity to reply at once or even to understand fully what he had said.

'Well?' he demanded.

'One – one could not take up arms against the King!' she gasped. Every day of her childhood training went into the making of that statement.

'Are you so sure that *is* the King, Lucia? Remember the story of the infant savaged by a wild sow? They say that the terrified nurse substituted a carter's son for the mutilated prince. In truth, Edward's tastes are those of a ditcher!'

'That is nonsense,' Lucia said briskly. 'Do you imagine that any mother would not know a strange child at her bosom?'

'Nevertheless, the Queen was worried by the story. Now, years later, we have this strange man called John, with scarred face and body, coming to Oxford, claiming to be the real heir. His resemblance to the old King is striking.'

'Bartholomew,' Lucia said, 'you are a man of great imagination and I love you dearly. But Edward is my anointed King and I will not have him slandered.'

'He is also a man, Lucia, and not one tenth the man that Lancaster is for his country!'

'*Lancaster*—'

'Yes. My friend.'

'You *know* this traitor who plotted with Scottish rebels?'

'That is untrue. He is a man of honour. I flew his colours aboard the *Gaillard* ten years ago, before the siege of Scarborough Castle.'

'Yours – was the spying ship?' She was very calm now, knowing the worst. 'You put Lancaster ashore after he watched the King depart?'

'Yes.'

'Then you murdered Piers Gaveston.'

'Lucia, will you listen to me? This might be the last time we will ever speak together. I brought you home so that you might be independent of me. You have shown me your choice. I will leave you as soon as I have told you what happened, and why.'

'I will hear you,' she said, 'and then you must go to join the traitor-earl. That was the purpose in your coming; that was why you kept your archers in battle-training all through the winter. Why disappoint Lancaster? You leave only a wife who loves you and a daughter who dotes upon you.'

He said, very low:

'If you loved me, you would try to understand, not *what* was done but *why* it was done. Yet this story begins in hatred, not love. My unhappy youth in Cleveland, Lucia, was destined to shape my entire life. It was here that I conceived my loathing for the le Latimers, to whom I was page and squire. I did not hate them for their treatment of me, but for growing rich in lands by appeasing the King. I watched them fighting under the royal standard for good or ill, jumping to obey every command – not for loyalty but for gain. And the sight sickened me. I watched your forced marriage with the younger William and anger gave me courage to help you run away. Anger and hate are the foundations of all that followed.

'Now, into the daily gossip of Hall and kitchens came

the name of the splendid and defiant Lancaster, already
virulent in his condemnation of the young Prince of Wales.
Here was a man I could respect.

'Fascinated, I followed the train of events by listening
to the conversations of my elders while I served their bread
or turned their meat upon spits. Lancaster was a rebel long
before the coronation of this Edward. And I made him my
hero.

'Well, the years passed. I ran away to London after
assisting you to rejoin your lover, Lucia. That event
matured me more than any other in my life. If I had taken
you for my own then, none of the rest would have
happened – for either of us. But we were too young, too
inexperienced. Now I was saddled with a hopeless love. I
never thought to see you again...

'The name of Lancaster became the one bright,
unmoving star in my firmament, the only alliance towards
which I could work with any hope of success.

'Five years in the Doge's army saw me grown into
manhood. Later, the sea brought me wealth, art brought
me prestige, but meanwhile, I had returned to France, and
soon afterwards sailed for England.

'Quite by chance, in the house of a friend in London, I
was introduced to the Earl of Lancaster. Hero and admirer
were face to face.

'After a while, he enquired of me:

' "Is it true that you have a ship?"

'I said that it was true, and he asked:

' "Is she good? Fast?" – and I replied that she had been
built in the Venetian Arsenal.

'He fell into deep thought, staring at me. His eyes were
like twin foxes, his nose sharp and fine-nostrilled as though
modelled by the wind.

' "Where are you bound for?" he asked suddenly, and I told him the north-east coast.

' "Trade?" he asked.

' "No."

' "What then?"

' "A pilgrimage I make occasionally for the good of my soul."

'He laughed and said:

' "There could be no better reason unless it were the welfare of England."

'Then he asked me to take wine with him privately later that night. I agreed gladly because I had not seen nearly enough of him: he interested and excited me. We repaired to another house and there he told me, in secret, of the recent meeting of the barons in St. Paul's, at which it was decided that Piers Gaveston, the King's favourite, must die.

'Now, it was against my every instinct to become a party to this, or to any other murder, but the Earl of Lancaster's hand was clamped over mine on the table and the twin fox eyes burned into my soul. I think then, Lucia, that he knew me exactly. He knew that I was an idealist – that all my life I had been seeking the right path and someone to guide me along it. Lancaster had all the strength of leadership; it remained only for him to convince me about the regularity of his aims. And I was willing to be convinced.

' "Help me, de Fanacourt," he said, "to save my country in the eyes of God. With Gaveston dead, Edward might yet be a man."

' "Why can Gaveston not be exiled instead?" I asked.

'Lancaster gave an angry snort.

' "He *has* been exiled – Edward has annulled it. He has been excommunicated – Edward has embraced him. Now,

I tell you, *he must die.* It will not be murder. He will be legally executed after a public trial."

'I considered it for a while, and then I said:

' "I will have no part of it" – and arose to leave. The Earl held me by the arm.

' "Will you not help to write history?" he demanded. "Will you disassociate yourself from the events of all countries because you yourself have none? Frenchman, Venetian, what are you? And have you never killed?"

' "Yes," I replied truthfully, "many times. But not murdered."

'Lancaster began to speak more calmly and patiently.

' "I have told you, it cannot be murder. Our aim is only to separate Gaveston long enough from Edward's side for him to be tried. Once tried, he will be found guilty because his crimes are publicly known and already proven. Guilty, he will be executed."

'Still I hesitated and Lancaster looked at me sharply.

' "Have you ever loved?" he enquired.

' "Once," I said.

' "Unhappily?"

' "Unsuccessfully."

' "Then," Lancaster said triumphantly, "there is nothing else for you except to throw yourself into whatever chance of adventure comes your way. I promise you excitement, comradeship and wealth. Are you with me?"

'A great ring gleamed on Lancaster's hand. I shut out the taper light from its stone by placing my fingers over it.

' "Good," Lancaster said. "Now, you will anchor off Tynemouth. Edward is in Newcastle and I will attack him there from the land. If he escapes, he will escape by sea. I want to follow him – in the *Gaillard*..." '

There was a long silence in Brotton's solar and Lucia sat unmoving, waiting for her husband to continue.

'I remember the sight of Newcastle-upon-Tyne burning under the dark sky, the flames reflected in the water as bales of wool in the dockside warehouses caught alight. I saw the royal ships fleeing in panic and disorder.

'My instructions were to wait for the pursuing Lancaster, but by the time the triumphant earl arrived, the *Gaillard* had missed the tide.

'Lancaster raved and cursed.

' "By our Lady," he said, "they'll be in Scarborough by this evening!"

'And so they were – Edward and Gaveston secure in the fortified castle above the town, an impenetrable, unassailable building.

'One half of my mind rejoiced that the quarry had escaped: the other half, already tuned to the noises of the chase, echoed Lancaster's blasphemies.'

'The *Gaillard* reached Scarborough and lay out of sight until nightfall. Meanwhile, Lancaster's victorious army marched from Newcastle to surround the fortress.

' "They'll have to come out," Lancaster said for the hundredth time. "I relieved them of horses, treasure, arms and food in Newcastle. They *must* come out."

'And Edward the King came, with a small company of chosen men—'

Lucia jumped up and faced her husband furiously.

'You realise that Sir Robert de Everingham was of that company, Bartholomew? One of the noblest men who ever wore armour...'

He avoided her eyes.

'I know it now, Lucia. But I did not know it then. If Sir Robert had been killed as a result of my action, I would never have approached you, whether you knew the truth or not. Please let me continue now to the end. The King and his men left the fortress under cover of darkness. They

used the cliff-face path and, once safely on the beach,
quickly dispersed in small boats. We, watching, knew that
they were gone to raise further troops throughout Yorkshire
and that they had left Gaveston within the castle, in the
belief that he was safe.

' "Now," Lancaster said, "I intend to prise my pearl
from the oyster. Put me ashore, de Fanacourt. Let me
rejoin my men. Your task is done and you have my thanks
and friendship for life. The *Gaillard* is a good ship," he
added, as one pats a dog to please its master. "Will you
come to me again if I send for you?"

' "If your messenger can find me," I replied, "and I can
reach you in time." It seemed a safe enough promise…

'I set the earl ashore in the darkness on a desolate
beach. We clasped hands in farewell and I felt the great
Lancaster ring pressing into my flesh. For an instant, I
wished that the brief contact with this man, in whose presence there was vitality and utter certainty, were not at
an end.

' "I will rejoin you, Lancaster, if you need me," I said.
Thus the promise was spoken again, spontaneously: now it
was binding.

'As the earl moved away, I saw dark shapes emerging
from behind bushes and boulders; the men of Lancaster's
army were on the march behind their leader. And I half-
envied them.

'I ordered the *Gaillard* to move out from the cliff face
and anchor beyond the harbour, for I feared that her back
might be broken if there was to be a siege. On the other
hand, I wanted to know what the outcome of this entire
business was to be.

'An hour – two hours of utter silence and darkness
went by. Once, a thin moon sailed from behind ragged
cloud and the fortress was shown black and toothed against

the sky. Was Gaveston sleeping in there, I wondered, or was he pacing the length and breadth of the castle, making sure every sentry was alert? Or was he straining his eyes for sign of Edward's return?'

'Suddenly, a ring of fire sprang up around the castle. Arrows hailed, swords clanked, the rhythmic boom of a battering ram shattered the night silence. Sea birds shrieked in alarm. Lancaster had attacked the fortress with every man and weapon at his command. He had chosen his hour well – it was about three o'clock in the morning when men are low-spirited and confused.

' "Surrender!"

'I heard the word clearly. During the next lull in the attack, I heard Lancaster's voice again:

' "Come out, Gaveston. I will not harm you."

'And again:

' "Spare the King's men, Gaveston. Come out."

'As the clouds sifted the dawn light over the sea, a flag of truce was run up over the battlements. The clamour ceased. I saw the glint of armour ascending the hill as Lancaster went up to claim his prisoner, and I spoke aloud to myself:

' "He promised not to harm Gaveston and he is a man of his word. Perhaps, one day, I shall see England strong and peaceful under a mature king and know that I helped to make her so."

'But my thoughts turned to you, Lucia, in the Baysdale nunnery, and I knew that you would disapprove of this night's work even before the terrible sequel to it was acted out.'

She did not speak for a while. Then—

'Gaveston was murdered,' she said. 'Dragged from his bed, secretly tried, publicly beheaded. For your part in the murder, Bartholomew, I could forgive you. You were young, you had little foresight. But now you intend to rejoin Lancaster on the strength of a ten-year-old promise, and to take up arms against the King. For this I can never forgive you, nor can I remain married to a traitor.

She went into her bed-chamber and drew the curtains close. She heard Bartholomew leave the solar and cross the Hall. After a while, the sound of his horse's hoofbeats grew fainter and fainter in the distance. He was gone.

17

'Where is the master, my lady?' Christina asked in surprise, looking around the solar.

'He has gone to York on urgent business,' Lucia lied.

It was the first of many lies she was to tell to explain Bartholomew's absence. At first, she lied through shame for what he was doing, but later through a deep fear for his safety: if it became known among the King's many supporters in Cleveland that de Fanacourt had rejoined the rebel Lancaster, they would hunt him out wherever he was hiding. Above all, she felt that she had to protect him from her loyal cousin, William de Thweng, a fanatic in the royal cause. Therefore, she avoided Kilton.

But, late one night, William visited Brotton.

'Lucia, where is Bartholomew?' he demanded as soon as they were alone.

'He went to York – I think…'

'Are you not certain, Lucia? I am in great haste for York myself. Thomas of Lancaster is massing an army somewhere along the borders of his estates and the King has summoned every baron to ride throughout the night with all their strength of men. Peter de Mauley is now assembling our combined forces.'

The urgency of his manner agitated her and she began to pace up and down the solar.

'What can all this have to do with Bartholomew? He is a foreigner—'

'We want him with us. That way, there can be no misunderstandings. And, besides, he has a band of trained archers which we need.'

'I have told you, William, he has already left here. He went many days ago and was not clear about his journey. I did not question him. Why should you question me now?'

'Because I have known for a long time that his sympathies are with Lancaster. Now the *Gaillard* lies unmanned at Whitby. The archers have been spirited way. My Lord Bartholomew de Fanacourt is not with his Lady at Brotton and it is obvious that she does not know where he is. Lucia' – he gripped her shoulders and she felt his breath upon her face – 'if your husband is with Lancaster, he is a dead man.'

Unnerved, she spoke quickly, without thinking.

'Dead? And why should *they* not win and you lose?'

The truth was out now and de Thweng shook his head angrily.

'Because I know their strength and I know they are outnumbered and already half-surrounded.'

'I see,' she said after a while. It was useless to keep up the pretence. 'What can I do, William? I love him. He is foolish and idealistic. He did not even want to go on this expedition, but felt himself bound by some old vow. It was his loyalty which I loved first. What can I do?'

'Come with me. Now, without delay. I have wasted too much time already and will explain as we ride. We will join de Mauley and the men.'

She snatched her leather coat from the petch and drew on her gloves while calling to a serving boy to have her horse brought out at once, and to Christina to see to the baby when she awakened. She was calmer now, every action economical of time. It was only when she walked outside into the sharp night air with William at her elbow that she asked the question uppermost in her mind.

'What is the purpose of my going?'

'You may be in time to dissuade him from taking action against the King. If he does it, and is captured, there will be no mercy. Edward has sworn that this battle is to be the avenging of Piers Gaveston's murder…'

A cold hand clamped about her heart. If Edward were to discover her husband's part in the siege of Scarborough Castle – She shut the thought out of her mind lest it communicate itself even to William de Thweng as, hurriedly, he helped her to mount.

'William,' she said gently, 'one moment more: why are you so concerned for a rebel?'

He glanced at her briefly in the starlight.

'You are too fine a woman to sleep alone, Lucia. Also, you have a child: I have none.'

It was a great pity that he had not, she thought, as they rode quickly away. His wife, Catherine, was losing her beauty and William himself had little interest in Kilton's castle or estates: a child – or many children, as in the old days – might have given some purpose to their lives.

It was a cold night under a hard, dry sky. There was no moon, but a million stars shone frostily on thin, crisp snow.

Lucia rode between de Mauley and de Thweng at the head of the men who were scattered out for a great distance behind. She could hear the murmur of their voices, the crunch of their horses' hooves, the occasional girlish giggle of a page excited by his first armed ride, the sharp sounds of weapons and armour jolting together.

William de Thweng was silent now, keeping himself apart, but de Mauley stayed close to Lucia. It was twenty years since they had met, and a little remaining vanity made her grateful to the darkness. She looked at him side-long and he appeared unaltered to her. He was still very thin, wore his lank hair long and rode in the untidy, indo-lent manner which had always been his way.

'You have not changed, Lucia,' he said suddenly.

'You cannot see me,' she laughed, surprised.

'I meant your presence. You are as vital as I remember.'

She sighed.

'I am not vital, Peter. You know why I am riding with you?'

'Yes. Do you think your husband will listen to you and be dissuaded?'

'If he does so,' she said, after a pause, 'I will honour him less, but his life is dearer to me than all honour.'

They did not speak again for several miles. The going was rough and difficult for the horses. On the next stretch of level ground, Lucia asked:

'Do you still hunt with Nicholas de Menyll, Peter?' – for the silence had become oppressive. 'I heard the pair of you were fined for poaching in Pickering Forest!'

Peter laughed briefly at the recollection.

'That was a long time ago. No, no one sees Nicholas now.'

'Why is that?' All at once she was deeply concerned about the wayward man who had fathered her second son.

De Mauley hesitated, sensing her concern.

'He was always a wild man, Lucia, as you well know. Now, it seems, he is a wild animal. He has deserted Whorlton and taken to the forests completely. He believes every man's hand to be against him and wages a private war on all comers. Rebels and Royalist alike thirst for his blood, and I fear he will come to a violent end. An outlaw's life is brief when he is alone.'

'Alone,' she echoed sadly, thinking that it need not have been so… 'And his great wolfhound, Cain, what became of him?'

'Cain leapt into an icy lake to bring a bird ashore that Nicholas had shot. He stiffened and drowned like a stone.'

Again they rode in silence until Peter drew close to her and touched her arm.

'What a bearer of ill-tidings I am,' he remarked contritely. 'You are truly sad now. Tell me one thing more, though, before we forget the sorry past: have you ever heard of Whorlton's heir, your son?'

'Oh, yes. Yes, indeed.' Her whole face lit up with pleasure and her eyes glowed. 'This winter past, in France. Bartholomew heard news of a youth called de Menyll in Calais and caused enquiry to be made. It was young Nicholas. My husband then arranged for me to journey there to meet the boy. He – he received me well.'

'By our Lady, so he ought!'

'He need not have,' she said simply. 'But he was courteous and gentle – perhaps a trifle tongue-tied, as youths will be, although I hardly noticed, I was so busy looking at him, clasping his hands, saying foolish things… Oh, Peter, he is so very handsome! His hair is like bunches of blue-black grapes. He resembles his father, when young, in all things except the mad light in the eye. Young Nicholas is gentle. When he bade me farewell, he seemed near to tears.'

She blew her nose energetically.

'It was kind of your husband,' Peter remarked, after some thought, 'to arrange the meeting.'

'Bartholomew is a kind and good man. That is why I want him back beside me and our infant daughter.'

'You have a daughter? Aha, I have a son – noisy and destructive – a vandal – the plague of my old age!' But the warmth of parental pride was in his voice when he said it and Lucia rejoiced for him sincerely. They discussed this small son at great length, and then Lucia's daughter, and compared them both in age and size and accomplishments, and wondered if they would ever meet…

The night wore on and gave place to a silver dawn and, after that, a fiery red sun shot one finger straight into the sky and the whole world was transformed into a shining, sparkling place.

'Halt!' William shouted. 'We will rest.'

'Halt – halt,' echoed voices for miles back. The men dismounted and began to tend their horses. The breaths of men and animals made silver clouds in the air and the frosty red sun cleared the highest hill.

Lucia felt neither weariness nor hunger nor need of the night's sleep she had lost. Her very instinct was to gallop forward, leaving the others behind. She must reach Bartholomew, reason with him, plead with him to give up this course of action. She blamed herself bitterly for not having tried before he left Brotton, for having sent him away from her so harshly.

Yet, in her heart, she knew that he would not be dissuaded either then or now. He had given his word voluntarily to Thomas of Lancaster long before he had taken her for his wife.

It was useless to go on. She did not even know where to

look for him except at Lancaster's side. Very well then, she must find Lancaster...

An hour after sunrise, a rider was sighted approaching in great haste. He wore the King's colours and was known to de Thweng, with whom he held earnest, hurried conversation alone. Then he rode away as he had come.

De Thweng beckoned Lucia and de Mauley to him, with some of the leading riders among the men.

'Lancaster is at Burg,' he said tersely. 'We can be there my midday. The King's forces under Sir Andrew de Harkeley are already in position outside the town, on the east bank of the River Ure.'

So, Lucia thought, *it is already too late. But I will still go on...*

She heard William and Peter shouting their orders to the men. She saw the far-flung ranks tighten and the direction of their progress alter to a more westerly course. Many of those men who had set out so confidently for York, there to join orderly forces with their King from Pontefract, would never see that fortified city, today nor any day. But the busy, self-contained little town sometimes called Burg, other times Boroughbridge, was to write its name in history and in blood. It was the eleventh day of April, 1322.

The royal forces were assembled on the river bank. Kilton and Mulgrave were assigned their positions. Reinforcements rode in from the south and, later, another small army from the north-west. It was a proud and confident and dedicated gathering in full battle array under the clear, pale sun. Before and below them lay the bridge spanning the snow-swollen River Ure.

And, beyond the bridge, at the far side of the town, Lancaster's army awaited the attack.

The inhabitants of Burg had either locked themselves inside their homes or had fled into the country. Not a dog roamed the narrow streets. There was no sound, no movement except a pair of wagtails skimming the icy waters of the Ure, and the standards flapping in the sunny wind.

The Commander raised his right arm, index finger extended. Before he had lowered it swiftly to the height of his shoulder, the King's army was pouring down into the town and thundering over the bridge. And, before it reached the far bank of the Ure, Lancaster's men charged. To the din of hooves and shouting and weapon-clashing was added the splash of men and horses falling into the water. After a short time, the water below the bridge turned a reddish brown and carried froth and foam upon it like an angry sea.

Backwards and forwards the battle raged, up and down narrow streets, over and back across the bridge. The royal reserve forces charged, but Lancaster too had reinforcements, and a new battle began.

Once only Lucia glimpsed Bartholomew and, although she was a long way off, she screamed a warning to him that an enemy archer had him in sight. As though he could have heard her, he reared his mount and the arrow passed its throat.

She strained her eyes for another sight of him until darkness fell, but did not see him.

Now lighted torches were added to the scene, and presently a house burst into flames and was mirrored in the river. The neighbouring dwelling caught fire, and then another house on the opposite bank, as the wind blew sparks and pieces of flaming wood and thatch. Against the blazing buildings, the black armies fought on until midnight had passed.

Some of Lancaster's men had hidden themselves under the structure of the bridge and, with their swords thrust through the gaps in the woodwork, injured many horses and men, including the Earl of Hereford.

A light snow began to fall in the early hours of the morning. The fires had almost died out and the noise subsided except for an occasional clash in side streets.

Lucia, numb and bewildered, did not even know how the battle had fared. For hours she had crouched with a group of towns-people in a little wood above the river, and all their gossip was only the wildest conjecture.

She heard her name being called. It was Peter de Mauley's voice and she stumbled towards him.

'Peter, what—?'

'Good tidings for some, Lucia,' he said, avoiding her eyes. 'Lancaster has been captured.'

'And Bartholomew?'

'He was with his leader to the last. We could not take the one without the other.'

'He is still alive?'

'Yes, but wounded. All prisoners are being taken to Pontefract at once. It is the King's order.'

'Help me mount then, Peter. I, too, am for Pontefract.'

He did not question her decision but said at once:

'I will lead you there.'

THE NORMAN CASTLE of Pomfret loomed black and forbidding against the rising sun and its shadow was long. The gates had been open since the first messenger arrived to tell the King of his victory, and now an endless stream of prisoners and captors entered while a fresh host of other riders galloped outwards.

De Mauley stopped one of these.

'Where are you going?' he demanded.

'I'm for Gloucester,' the rider told him hurriedly. 'Others have gone ahead at first light – for Bristol, Cardiff, Winchelsea and Windsor. There are to be executions all up and down the country this day. Every rebel is to be killed…'

Lucia put her hand to her eyes.

'Come, Peter,' she said, 'there is still time.'

They were admitted to a lower room of the castle and they sent an immediate message desiring audience of the King, but the servant who bore the message never returned. The large room was crowded with men, some having wounds attended to, others eating and drinking where they stood, and talking loudly of the great victory and the greater purge of rebels which was to follow.

'Now Gaveston is avenged, heh?' someone shouted, but he was quieted at once by his companions. In a lower tone, he went on, 'D'you know who they're waiting for now? For Her Majesty the Queen! She sent her command to Edward that Lancaster was not to be tried until her coming. Tried! Hah, that's a good story, isn't it?'

All the men laughed.

'Edward will have the Fiddler's head by morning, Isabella or no…'

Then someone asked, puzzled:

'Why should the Queen plead for Lancaster?'

A wink travelled around among the knowing ones.

'Because,' said the first speaker, very low, 'whatever the King is against, his Queen is for and t'other way round!'

'You mean she was on the side of the rebels?'

'No, no, no. She has her own fish to fry – eh, friends? Forget what I said. Remember only that Thomas of Lancaster has royal blood in his veins.'

Sickened, Lucia went outside and stood in the April sunshine. She was faint from hunger and exhaustion but could not eat the food which Peter fetched for her because there was a feeling of obstruction in her throat.

After a long time, William de Thweng came out of the castle and walked quickly to where she and Peter were standing.

'I have tried to speak to the King about Bartholomew,' he said, 'but he will not hear me. Everything is being held up now until after Lancaster's trial. We can do no more.'

'When will the trial be?' Lucia asked faintly.

'This evening or tonight. When the Queen arrives.'

William looked sharply at his cousin. In the sunlight her face had a transparent quality, and there was a fragility about her which he had never thought possible. Her eyes were large and dark-circled and the golden flecks had been absorbed into a kind of blackness. He saw the uncontrollable shaking of her hands.

'Wait for me here,' he said abruptly and vanished within again. After a while, he reappeared with a servant at his heels.

'There is a small apartment at your disposal, Lucia. I beg of you to go and rest there. De Mauley and I will continue our efforts on Bartholomew's behalf and will come for you as soon as we obtain audience.'

Blindly, she followed the servant indoors and through a maze of passages to a little cell-like room where no noise penetrated. She lay down on a palliasse in the corner. Sleep came upon her at once.

SHE AWOKE to see a lighted taper in the room and an old woman sitting sewing. There was no confusion in her mind concerning her whereabouts or the length of time she had slept. She knew that it was almost dawn, and the night-

mare of Bartholomew's plight was upon her even before
she opened her eyes.

'Is the trial of the Earl of Lancaster over?' she asked
the old retainer who had risen to her feet.

'Not yet, my lady. The doors have been barred since
sundown when the Queen arrived.'

'Has anyone enquired for me here?'

'The Baron de Thweng. He said you were not to be
awakened.'

'Then there is no news.' She flung back the coverings
and surveyed the dress in which she had slept. It was made
of fine wool and had not crumpled badly. The old woman
began to dress her hair for her with a soothing rhythmic
motion after she had bathed herself in a little bowl of rose-
water. Food and wine was laid ready, and she ate deter-
minedly so as not to feel faint again throughout the
long day.

A grey light was creeping in at the high narrow
window, and she wondered if Bartholomew was watching
this dawn and if he felt cold with fear and apprehension, as
she did. She wondered how badly wounded he had been,
and whether he was in pain. All the while she was thinking,
she was fastening her leather coat and crumpling her gloves
between her palms to warm them.

It was then that a shout rang through Pomfret Castle
which froze the blood in her veins. It was a sound made by
many throats, a savage animal noise, long drawn out and
terrible.

She tore aside the door curtain and ran into the corridor, trying to remember the way out. The shouting continued, leading her onward until she reached the lower room
by the entrance. Here, an even greater crowd of men than
on the previous day were jostling and making a great noise,

and all their eyes were fixed on a curtained stairway mounting to the private apartments.

William de Thweng was standing by the outer door and she pushed her way towards him. He put an arm protectively around her and held her shoulders against his chest so that she would not be trampled nor swept away by the movement of the crowd.

'Lancaster is to die,' he said in her ear. 'The Queen's plea on his behalf failed, but because of his royal blood he is to be spared some details of a traitor's death. He is with his confessor now.'

She turned her face upward towards her cousin so that he should hear her above the din.

'How many of his followers were executed yesterday?'

'Hundreds. But there is no news of Bartholomew, and Lancaster is to be the first victim here in Pontefract. There is still time, Lucia. Look, here is the procession.'

Down the steps clanked an armed guard, followed by the executioner. Then came a priest garbed all in black with a gold cross at his breast and, behind him, a tall thin man still wearing the close-fitting garments which had padded his armour.

'Lancaster!' yelled the waiting men but, afterwards, they were strangely silent as the Earl moved down the floor towards them, followed by another and a stronger guard.

He was within three feet of Lucia when he raised his eyes and her horrified stare drew his gaze. His eyes were light blue and clear as ice above the high fine-nostrilled nose and the gaunt cheekbones. Impatiently, he looked away at once, thinking her a spectacle-seeker, but as he passed she whispered:

'God give you courage. You have many friends' – and he bowed his head towards her. She had spoken the words for Bartholomew's sake, knowing that he would wish them said, but also because as a woman the sight of this man walking alone towards a bloody death was terrible to her, and her compassion for him was great. She felt his hopelessness, his isolation.

Now the crowd pushed forward, forcing her and William down the steps. He managed to pull her out of the main stream and they retreated together towards the far wall of the courtyard where the night-fallen snow was untrampled.

The gates were now opened and a screaming horde of townspeople rushed inside and were roughly handled by the men-at-arms who ordered them back. After some delay and the landing of several blows, the centre of the courtyard was cleared except for the procession and an old, unharnessed grey horse, winded and broken-kneed. On to this animal's back the Earl of Lancaster was hoisted, for, his hands being bound, he could not mount unaided.

The people and the guards laughed uproariously at this reversal of a man's fortunes: Thomas of Lancaster had owned, until this morning, the finest horses in England. Now all his goods and property were forfeit.

Someone threw a handful of snow which hit the grey animal on the ear, but when it only bowed its head wearily and made no movement, everyone laughed the more. Many people were now arming themselves with snowballs in preparation for the moment when Lancaster would pass by for the last time…

'Oh, God,' Lucia wept, 'cannot they give death even a little dignity?'

The procession was ready to move off, the guard in place, the executioner fortified with wine, when a soldier rode forward carrying a battered, felted wool hat, and placed it on Lancaster's head. The hat was much too large for the prisoner and it slipped forward over his eyes, in which position it remained while he rode away, to the huge delight of the watchers.

But, to Lucia, that hat was a royal falcon's hood, slipped on to blind the too-seeing eyes beneath. It was in that moment that she understood the love her husband had borne this man, who was more regal than the King.

The last guard rode out of the gate and the people surged behind, taking their noise with them to the place of execution. On the steps of Pomfret Castle stood the group of sober men who had helped pass judgement but would not demean themselves to watch it carried out. At their forefront was Edward, with Isabella beside him.

18

Lucia stumbled across the slushed cobbles. The group on the steps of Pomfret was already retiring indoors out of the cold, and Isabella was saying something to the King through clenched teeth before she, too, turned away, casting him a glance of unremitting hatred.

Edward stood alone. He seemed unmindful of the cold, as though his whole attention were fixed on something else, a long way off.

Lucia kneeled in the icy mud and clasped her hands at his feet.

'My lord—'

He started and looked down. There was no flicker of recognition in his eyes.

'Who are you?' he enquired irritably.

'The former Lucia de Thweng, my Sovereign, now married to Bartholomew de Fanacourt.'

If she were altered as much as Edward was, it was not surprising that he failed to remember her. There was no trace now of the splendid young king who once rode into Whorlton. His face was that of a haggard, bitter man, and his gestures were quick and nervous as though he lived in constant fear for his life.

'Arise, arise, lady. What do you require with us?' His attention was still on a distant point outside Pomfret's gates.

'The life of my husband.'

'Indeed? Do we keep him?'

'He is your prisoner since yesterday.'

Now Edward became fully aware of the situation.

'You mean that you choose this moment to beg mercy for a rebel's follower? Indeed, my lady, your own indiscretions are well known and equally well remembered, but it seems to us that your husband has outdone them all in a few hours of fighting.'

She bowed her head before the blast of sarcasm. It was useless to plead with one so embittered.

'I had thought,' she said, very low, 'that some recollection of happier times might stir your royal memory. You patted my son's head once on an evening outside Whorlton Castle.'

'Whorlton... Lucia de Thweng.' For a moment his expression softened and, reaching out, he took her hand. 'We thank you for that time of gaiety when our friends were about us and our future without a cloud. Now—'

A great and distant shout reached Pomfret. The King's eyes narrowed and his lips smiled, transforming his expression from kindness to cruelty.

'Lancaster is dead!' he exulted. 'Ten years ago we dug his grave and that of his followers in a great ditch around Clarendon Castle...'

He turned swiftly to go indoors, but Lucia's cry was so full of defeat and hopelessness that he paused, gathering his robe in one hand.

'Why should we spare de Fanacourt?' he demanded.

'We are not unjust. He was the man who defended our enemy to the last.'

'Loyalty – bravery – they are no sins!' she cried, trying to hold him for another moment. One word now could tip the balance either way, and she prayed God that word be not Scarborough. 'I beg not pardon for him but only exile forever. Others have escaped to France, to Italy. Let him go and I will be his keeper forever in a foreign land.'

Again he was turning away. She raised her voice.

'My king, I beseech you not to orphan a little child!'

He stopped in mid-stride, his back towards her, and spoke over his shoulder.

'You have a child?'

'An infant. At my manor house in Brotton.'

The king flexed and unflexed his fingers. Children were dear to him. He could bear the hatred in his wife's eyes; soon he was to bear inhuman treatment of his own person; but never a threat to a child's future. Unwittingly Lucia had put her finger, gently, on this royal weakness, as others were to do later, but with malice.

'Your husband was taken to York last evening with other prisoners,' the King said. 'You will receive an Order of Release into Exile for him. Ride with it to our Commander at York and God lend you speed.'

SHE CARRIED the King's Order inside her dress, where its rough edges pricked her skin like a goad.

The journey to York, with William de Thweng galloping beside her, had all the qualities of pursuit in a nightmare: the body stretched forward, straining towards its goal, while everything conspired to hold it back.

Fear of further delay made the heart pound. She

wanted to urge the horses forward with whip and spur, and yet watch every rut in the road lest they break a leg. She wanted to take short cuts across country, but feared marshy ground from the snows and the necessity of turning back on to the main highway.

Several times William tried to speak to her but without success. She was convinced that conversation of any kind would slow their pace.

The city of York was her goal. Once within its gates, she believed that her mission would be almost over. The Commander would be found without delay. He would honour the King's Order.

But York, on this April evening, was not a city she recognised. It was a teeming, undisciplined ant-heap where even admission within its outer fortification had to be disputed.

'Let us pass, I say!' thundered William de Thweng to a group of soldiers barring their way. After unhurried consultation, the soldiers moved aside and leered at Lucia, touching her as she passed. They were drunk with wine, victory and the smell of blood.

William and Lucia fought their way past Maudlin Spittal. Outside the Hospital of St. Mary Magdalen there was a rioting mob. Further down Chapel Lane and all the way to Lady Mill, the route seemed entirely blocked. They had to go back to try and reach the city centre by another road.

At last they were in the narrow streets leading to the Norman Minster. Revellers, layabouts, priests, soldiers, country people in for the day's spectacle, all combined to form a seething, impassable mass.

'This way,' William said grimly, turning his horse down a pitch-dark alley entirely roofed over with vegetation where the citizens of York had been dumping their rubbish for months until it was knee-high and stinking. He dismounted into the quagmire and led both horses.

Somehow, they emerged near the castle, by the new dams of the River Foss.

'We will ask first at the gates if the King's Commander is within.'

They waited for an answer to their enquiry. No answer came except the sounds of drunken mirth from within. They sent another, and another message. They paid a retainer in gold to find the Commander for them, promising more gold when he had done so, but he was content with the first payment and never returned. They questioned uninterested soldiers who neither knew nor cared where their Commander was spending his evening. It was like searching for one human being among a drunken million.

At last, William rode away alone and came back leading an elderly peasant by the ear.

'This fellow swears that the Commander is housed in a tent outside the Old Baile building. If he lies, I'll slit his throat.'

They set off for the Old Baile, and it was now very late, but York was wide awake and noisy and obstructive as before. William bawled at the full strength of his lungs at anyone who got in his path – or failed to get out of it quickly enough – for he was tired and irritated beyond measure. He used his whip extensively and finally rode with drawn sword.

They reached the Old Baile and were confronted by two sentries.

'Nobody must pass until morning…'

William filled his lungs with the midnight air.

'The Baron de Thweng of Kilton,' he roared, 'comes

direct from our King at Pontefract with Orders for your Commander. *Lead us to him!*'

They did not argue further. One of them ran ahead immediately, beckoning and pointing.

'The Commander's tent.'

'At last!' Lucia sobbed.

There was a light burning inside the tent and the flap was open, although it was a cold night. Inside she could see a long table littered with documents.

'Lucia – one moment.' William held her back. 'There is something I have wished to tell you all day. You must know it now. The King's Commander here in York is your former husband, le Latimer of Danby.'

She felt the strength drain out of her body.

'He – could not defy the King's Order?'

'No, but he could delay it until – Be tactful with him, Lucia, if it is indeed he, and not some deputy, who is within the tent.'

She walked alone towards the open flap and another sentry stepped forward, to whom she told her name and business. She could hear a low murmur of voices, question and answer. Then the sentry came out again.

'The Commander has retired for the night and is not to be disturbed. You are to leave the Order for his attention in the morning.' The sentry held out his hand.

'I will not let the Order out of my sight,' Lucia cried desperately, drawing back from him. 'Whoever occupies Sir William le Latimer's place within must peruse the document in my hand.' Her voice had grown loud with panic and, out of the corner of her eye, she saw her loyal cousin moving closer to her in the darkness.

Then, from inside the tent, an unfamiliar voice said:

'Let her come in.'

She stooped to enter and, for the moment, was blinded by the light and smoke from a wick floating in a bowl of oil. Then, seated behind the littered table, she saw a fair-haired man of about thirty years or less. He had pale eyes and a pink complexion. He did not rise when she approached him, but, finger on chin, watched her unblinkingly.

'Let me see the Order,' he commanded brusquely.

Her hands fumbled with the fastenings of her coat and he continue to watch her, without sympathy, without offer of help. She drew the document out of the bosom of her dress and held it out for his inspection. Swiftly, he took it away from her, and she stifled a cry of protest.

'Ummm, "Release into Exile",' he quoted, smiling. "That means that you, too, by accompanying the prisoner, would forfeit all your property to the Crown?'

'The property has dwindled to a mere nothing,' she replied, 'through neglect and – theft. But were my inheritance still in its original abundance, I would give it all willingly for my husband's life.'

'He must be very dear to you,' the fair-haired man said mockingly. 'But then, you always paid extravagantly for your lovers, did you not, and disregarded your children?'

She knew him now, and the recognition shocked her.

'You are my first-born?'

'Yes. But, I pray you, do not call me son.'

'I feel no desire to do so. By some strange alchemy, you resemble my late father-in-law more than anyone.'

'Then perhaps you would tell me, lady whore, who was my own real father, that I may strive to look as he did?' He had risen from his seat and was leaning across the table towards her. An almost tangible hatred hung between them – his, nurtured with spite throughout the years, hers born only a few moments previously out of dislike, anger and outrage.

She struck him fiercely.

'You are unworthy to be even a bastard of de Thweng!'

He straightened to his full height, but was not as tall as she.

'You will regret that blow,' he said softly.

He moved to the bowl of oil with the lighted wick in it out of her reach and then held the precious document over the naked flame. She lunged for it wildly, but the table was broad and solid. Her screams brought her cousin and the sentry running.

'The Order – he is burning it…'

De Thweng flung himself upon the youngest le Latimer and the sentry set about de Thweng. Other men-at-arms rushed in and joined the fight on whichever side appealed to them. Panting, le Latimer extricated himself and faced his mother, brandishing the charred document before her face.

'It would still be legal,' he shouted, 'if de Fanacourt were alive. But, early this morning, his head was hacked from his body—'

A rush of red sparks pricked the sudden darkness before her eyes and she had the sensation of falling into a pit. When the darkness cleared, a strange, elderly man was leaning over her, making ineffectual clucking noises with his tongue. He had a mane of rough grey hair and he was very fat.

They looked at each other without hostility, without friendship, these two who had once been husband and wife. For Lucia, William le Latimer, the King's Commander at York, was merely someone she had known a long time previously, now more than half-forgotten.

'We sought for you all day, William,' she said wearily. 'Now it is too late.'

She heard her cousin say:

'Lucia, there has been a mistake.'

'A mistake?'

'Yes. The Commander will explain.

Le Latimer was shuffling through the documents on the table. He ran a black-nailed finger down a long list of names and titles.

'Lady de Fanacourt,' he mumbled then, 'ah – Lucia, your husband, Bartholomew, was badly wounded. I – er – considered him unfit to stand trial. He is being cared for in the prison nearby.'

As soon as the meaning of the words reached her, she turned her head slowly to look at her son. He lowered his gaze before hers and walked out of the tent.

'I thank you, William,' she said simply, to the Commander. 'Your mercy, as much as the King's, has saved his life. Will you honour the charred Order?'

'Of course. Enough of it remains to bear my seal.'

He busied himself with the document and Lucia remained motionless, staring before her. She felt neither surprise, nor relief, nor gratitude. Perhaps these things would come later when she had seen and touched her husband.

Now le Latimer was placing the Order in her hand, folding her limp fingers over it awkwardly. She heard him calling to his sergeant. She felt William de Thweng's guiding hand on her arm…

'Let us go, Lucia…'

The sergeant's keys were ringing Bartholomew's freedom.

ALSO BY ELEANOR FAIRBURN

The White Seahorse

The Golden Hive

Crowned Ermine

The War of the Roses Quartet:

The Rose in Spring

White Rose, Dark Summer

The Rose at Harvest End

Winter's Rose

Writing as Catherine Carfax:

A Silence with Voices

The Semper Inheritance

To Die A Little

The Sleeping Salamander

Writing as Anna Neville:

House of the Chestnut Trees

Writing as Emma Gayle:

Cousin Caroline

Frenchman's Harvest

Writing as Elena Lyons:

The Haunting of Abbotsgarth

A Scent of Lilacs

READ ON FOR A PREVIEW OF 'THE WHITE SEAHORSE'

Connacht, Ireland, 1537

Graunya O Malley ... Born of the sea. From the rugged west coast of Ireland to the power-crazed court of Elizabeth I, Graunya O'Malley sails her fleet and commands her men – with fierce determination.

The White Seahorse charts not only the life of the legendary 'Graunuaile' – queen to some, and pirate to others – but the fate of the Irish tribes that she tried to protect against the growing might of the English Empire under Elizabeth Tudor. Two powerful women, as yet unaware of each other's existence, shared a unique conviction: that in an age of Reformation, war and politics, a woman can be both strong and vulnerable, but it is dangerous to love...

THE WHITE SEAHORSE

The September tides were running silver with herring.
From every hump-backed island in Clew Bay the black
curraghs were launched, and their high prows pointed
westward towards the open Atlantic. They dipped their
nets and gathered the shining, gasping harvest while sea-
birds screamed and circled overhead.

Across the wide mouth of the bay stretched Clare
Island, one thousand five hundred and twenty feet high, a
fortress battered by the ocean. The air was so clear today
that the curraghmen could see the sunlit strand, and the
huddled dwellings, and the summer residence of O Malley
on Clare although it was thirteen miles distant from
Murrisk.

Owen O Malley of the Black Oak, lord of Upper
Umall, was watching his catch being landed. He saw the
herring not as fish but as currency: topped, tailed and
salted, packed in barrels and shipped to Spain and Portu-
gal, the 'chicken of the sea' would bring back, by
exchange, wines and spices, nails, iron and copper, alum,
fruit and Grains of Paradise. Owen O Malley was a rich

man in this year of fifteen hundred and thirty-seven, as well as being chief of wide territories on the mainland and among the other islands southward from Clare to Inishbofin.

His steward came striding up, bare-chested, from the beach, sand caking his feet and legs like boots. He bellowed in Irish, 'O Maulya, they're all in now. A fine harvest, praise be to God. Will there be another run, do you think?'

The chief fingered his long brown beard and stroked the whiskers on his upper lip. He looked out to sea with mild grey eyes from which the Viking fires of his remote ancestors had died, leaving only a wealth of knowledge.

'No,' he said, 'no, the shoals will turn north before evening. We have enough without chasing them and, maybe, running into trouble with O Donnell of the Fish. Get the salting started.'

'At once, O Maulya.'

'I'd like to leave for Spain three days from now if the weather is right. You attend to the catch, O Toole. I'll prepare the fleet myself.'

'You'll head straight for Biscay?'

'Aye: La Coruña. Then, if there's no swell, south to Vigo.'

The man plunged off down to the strand again, where the entire island population was noisily gathered. Girls and women in saffron-dyed petticoats were hauling the dripping creels of fish up out of the sea's reach to where a circle of old men worked with knives, gutting and cleaning. Farther up, on the short, cropped grass that was vivid green from dampness, salters and packers were busy. There was speed and rhythm here, a fusion of light-hearted noise and crude colour against the heaving grey backdrop of the ocean.

O Malley considered the scene for a moment longer,

then began to climb towards Knockmore. He wanted to study the empty Atlantic, from whence came the prevailing winds, the sou'westerlies; and he wanted to read the sky as far in advance as he could before taking his trading fleet out under the Blue Ensign. Weather was almost a religion here, and the signs and omens were interpreted by the chieftain as if by a high priest.

The mountain towered on his right side, seeming loftier and more sheer because of the smallness of the marshy island which it dominated. Rare birds nested in its upper crannies and strange plants grew on the south and east faces – there was always colour here, brilliant or delicate, flashing in movement or caught in utter stillness against the blue slate and the grey limestone – but, to the west, was only complete barrenness, a sheer cliff wall of rock frowning down on an ocean, which seethed and boiled and pounded even on the calmest day.

As he climbed, the sky spun away dizzily…

Now he paused, winded, and looked behind and down. A small figure in a white smock was following him. He circled his mouth with strong square hands.

'Graunya!' he shouted. 'Graunya, go back!'

She looked up briefly and continued to climb. Obedience had never been a strong point with Graunya O Malley in all her nearly-eight years and, as the daughter of the chieftain, it had seldom been enforced upon her – the Lady Margaret, her mother, being the mildest of women.

The O Malley braced his back against a rock and waited for her, arms folded across his goatskin tunic, short sturdy legs tensed inside their rough wool braes. When the child looked up again, her father seemed menacingly solid as though he were part of the mountain; but she struggled towards him, her mouth slightly open from the effort of breathing.

Expressionlessly, he watched her dogged progress. She was small for her age, fine-boned with the enduring fragility of the thorntree. Her colouring was much darker than his, with no trace whatever of the early Viking blood: hair so black that it had a metallic blueness in the high-lights of the curls; skin which bronzed easily from sun and wind; eyes intensely dark with a black circle around the iris.

Panting, she came abreast of him, and gave a little grunt of triumph. In spite of her disobedience, he caressed her.

'Graunya, I told you to go back,' he said in Spanish. She was learning the language from the Grey Sisters on the island during the summer, and from the friars at Murrisk in the winter; her father spoke to her in Spanish whenever he could although he had only a merchant's knowledge of it himself.

She sniffed at the leather sheath of the hunting-knife in his kriss, then touched it with the tip of her tongue like a small inquisitive animal.

'I knew that you would not begin until you reached the summit,' she said.

'Begin to do what?'

'Judge the weather.'

'I must be alone when I do it. You have been told not to interrupt me.'

'I will be quiet.' She knew that the gift of weather prophecy was lodged by God Himself with the O Malley chieftains.

'So let us go on.' The father held out his hand to the child. 'Why did you come after me?'

'I heard O Toole telling them on the strand that you were sailing in three days.'

'Well?'

'I want you to take me with you.'

'*No.*'

'Why?'

'You're too young. Not yet turned eight years—'

'I can handle an oar as well as my brothers can.'

'That may be. But you're going to stay with your mother nevertheless. There's more to running a trading fleet than pulling an oar in the galleys. The high seas can be dangerous in more ways than one, and this is always a hurried trip in the autumn to beat storms and early darkness. Anyhow, you'd be in the men's way: that mane of hair would blow across their eyes!'

He gave it a playful tug and glanced sidelong at her face as he did so; instantly the underlip stuck out above the long chin, and the brows frowned.

'I'll cut it off,' she said, a growl in the back of her throat.

'Fine sight you'd look then. The women would lock you up until it grew. Now, have sense, Graunya. When you're older, I'll take you to France or Spain with me and you can choose cloth and lace for your clothes; you'd like that?'

But she wasn't listening. A huge moth had alighted on her forearm and she was absorbed in its splendid markings. Then she stumbled, and the moth fluttered away on a northward slant, higher and higher against the dazzling silver sky. She watched it out of sight, standing motionless with her head raised. Without warning, she said, 'I can see thunder…'

The O Malley looked at her sharply with narrowed eyes. More than once, of late, he had suspected that the gift of weather prophecy had fallen to his daughter and not to his sons. If this were indeed so, it would be a terrible thing, for no woman could be elected to the chieftainship and no chief could survive without the gift.

'There will be no thunder,' he said harshly.

The White Seahorse

The intense eyes searched his face, then slid away unblinking to the distant mountains that ringed the bay, from Mweelrea to Nephin Beg and around to the summit of Croaghaun in Achill...

She turned around and began to scramble down the steep slope, running and jumping like a goat.

He sighed, and walked over to the White Rock – the sacred stone where O Malley chieftains were inaugurated – which faced the Achill peninsula to the north. The entire northern skyline shimmered in a haze of moist heat. Behind Croaghaun, other mountains marched, paler and paler blue, fading to infinity. It was a scene of utter peace until, suddenly, above the farthest rampart, he saw the beginnings of a pillared cloud formation which was the cradle of an infant storm ... Half an hour previously it had not been visible; now he felt its pressure.

He lowered his hand to his kriss, an instinctive move-ment when he was disturbed, to feel the solidity of his hunting-knife. The sheath was empty.

'Oh, damn that child!' he roared in the language of his fathers, and began to crash down the path she had beaten.

There was no sign of Graunya on the strand when he reached it and, presently, he forgot about her in the urgency of other matters: the fish packing would have to be got under cover in case heavy rain fell and ruined the salt: stores already going aboard the ships would have to be protected too; several hours' work...

It was thunder-dark when he reached the low stone-built summer-house. Before he crossed the threshold he became aware of the commotion within. The rare sound of his wife's voice raised in anger halted him.

'Margaret—'

She looked up at him distractedly, and dismissed her serving women. Her fair skin was blotched with frenzied weeping and her corn-gold hair stuck out in wisps under the folded white linen kerchief. He put his arms around her shoulders and she began to weep again.

'Margaret, in God's name, what has happened?'

'We'll have to spend the entire winter here,' she wailed. 'We can't go back to Belclare or Cahirnamart. Graunya—'

'*Graunya?*' Remembering the knife, he went rigid with fear. 'What has she done? Speak to me, speak!'

The Lady Margaret stopped crying, and said with deathly calm,

'She has cut off all her hair.'

He choked a bellow of laughter and turned it into a cough; evidently this matter was very serious to the womenfolk although he could not see the full tragedy of it himself.

'*All* of it?' he asked in a funereal tone; and Margaret blinked away fresh tears.

'Have you ever known Graunya to do anything by halves?' she demanded, her voice rising, defying him to argue. He shook his head. 'Well,' his wife continued, 'She's shaved it to the skull. *With a knife!* God knows how she didn't cut her head off ... At any rate, we can't take her back to the mainland looking like that; people would think she was a leper.'

'Then there's only one cure for the situation,' he said.

'What is that?' – hopefully.

'I'll take her to Spain with me in the trading fleet. Donald can stay at home to make space for her – he shames us all with sea-sickness anyway! We'll be away nearly two months. By the end of that time, she will be presentable enough. Now, go and fetch her for me, Margaret; I want to see how bad it is.'

The sky outside had grown blue-black and huge drops of rain were beginning to fall. There was a scampering of

feet on the shingle path; the door burst open and the two
O Malley sons, Cormac and Donald, tumbled into the
apartment. At the same moment, the Lady Margaret
appeared at the opposite entrance, grasping her scowling
daughter by the hand.

The boys' wrestling match froze into paralysis. They
stared speechlessly at their sister. Then Cormac, the elder,
laughed shakily and cried, "Graunya! Graunya *mhaol*…"

The word meant anything from 'bare' to 'tonsured' and
he pronounced it *way-ull* in the fullness of the island
dialect. The instant after he had spoken, a flash of green
light illuminated the strand with unearthly brilliance; then
thunder shook the house.

The boys began to caper about, shouting, 'Graunya
mhaol! Graunya-mhaol—' until they were made aware of
their father's presence.

'Get out,' he said to them quietly, and they slipped like
river rats into the rear kitchens. 'Graunya, come here
to me.'

She was too horrified by the results of her handiwork,
and by the jeers of her brothers, to be able to cry. She felt
naked, plague-stricken and quite unaccountably cold. She
stared at her father with eyes so big and black that he
thought of rock pools fringed with shining seaweed, but
she expected him to recoil from the sight of her. Instead he
reached out a hand and patted the spiked tufts which the
knife had missed. She never loved him more than in that
moment…

'Graunya,' he said, 'there are people in this world
who will have what they want, whatever the price. You
are one of them. Fair enough! I'll take you to Spain with
me in order to save your lady mother from embarrassment—'

'You'll *take* me? The day after tomorrow?' She could

hardly believe it. She vibrated with anticipation like a plucked string.

'I have said so, and I will do it although it is against my will. It seems the only means of getting you out of the way. But remember this, Graunya, before we set out: the men of the fleet are likely to hit on the same nickname for you as your brothers have done. It may hurt: you deserve that. And it may stick for the rest of your life … I advise you to become accustomed to the sound of it.'

'Yes, my father,' she said, very meekly.

'Graunya mhaol! Graunya-mhaol. Graunuaile—' Like all words repeated, they ran together and lost their meaning.

Outside, across the bay, stretched a really spectacular rainbow.

On the night before undertaking a long sea journey, the O Malley always ate a meal with his men. Because the summer house on Clare Island was small, this could never be a feast in the mainland tradition – where two hundred people might crowd under one roof at Belclare or Cahir-namart – but the islanders liked to sit under the sky anyway, whatever the weather. They grouped themselves around the chieftain's residence, while he and his captains and his family dined within.

The newly caught herrings were sampled, slow-baked in earthenware ovens; then more substantial fare was brought – spit-roasted venison, beef and mutton followed by dripping honey-cakes washed down with ale and wine.

O Dugan the Baard sang, recounting deeds of dead heroes…

Owen O Malley was well aware of his own failings as a

chief. He knew that young men outside regarded his trading as a shamefully mild occupation, and that they blamed him for keeping them so engaged, wasting the years of their youth and vigour when they should be fighting. A man had to fight to prove his masculinity, and some of the island youths were having to quarrel amongst themselves for want of another enemy; they were too young to remember the great – and futile – battles of Owen O Malley's own succession of chieftainship, since when he had lived a life of determined amiability. Indeed, there was no prospect of any further bloodshed until the next *tanist*, or success to the title, was elected.

O Malley felt their resentment as surely as he had felt the pressure of the coming thunderstorm. He knew that he had to act, now, before leaving for Spain; otherwise, there was liable to be trouble in his absence.

'Let my eldest son come and sit by me,' he commanded, and the captains shuffled on their bench – where they crouched, facing the entrance, their shields hung behind them in time-honoured manner – to make room for him.

Cormac moved up from his low seat at the end of the board, where he had been sitting between his younger brother and Graunya, the latter wearing a felted wool cap pulled down over her ears. He was a lad of about twelve years, fair like his mother, open-faced and honest. The brehon law of his country recognised no birthright for him to succeed his father in the chieftainship. The chief was elected by the people from any member of the ruling family. Thus, they could pass over a weakling elder son to elect his more robust brother or cousin, or even uncle; this freedom of choice was fiercely defended by the clans.

But Owen O Malley was fairly certain that his son, Cormac, would be chosen as his own tanist.

'I wish to put this youth before you,' he said now, 'as my heir. If there are other candidates, let ye bring them forward in due time.'

The captains leapt up and shouted the news to the crowd outside. Instantly, there was uproar. O Malley listened carefully to the tone of it. After a while he leaned back against the wall, relaxed: it was a friendly commotion. He exchanged a glance with the Lady Margaret, who smiled and nodded her veiled head, content that all was going well. Cormac would be elected tanist. He would choose his personal army from among the restless young men and would spend several years training with them. That would keep them all out of mischief until the day of the traditional raid on some unfortunate neighbour's cattle...

Now everyone was shouting for the poet-harper.

'Let O Dugan sing! Let him sing!'

'And what would you have me to sing?' asked the bard.

'The *Thaw-in*!' they yelled. 'The Cattle Drive of Cooley.'

It was a predictable choice, that of the greatest epic in the Irish language; a story that began in comedy, continued in majesty, ended in stark tragedy.

Graunya had heard it many times before; it was already part of the fabric of her consciousness, a thing familiar although not fully understood in its deeper implications, an emotional experience shared. Her response to it was an echo of her clan's response: when they cheered, she did likewise; when they wept, tears ran down her cheeks.

She clasped her small hands together in her lap as the first notes of the little eight-stringed harp rippled like water running over smooth stones. O Dugan's voice sang:

> 'Maeve, the Queen of Connacht, was very
>   beautiful;
> But she was arrogant and jealous also.
> By her side lay Aillil, the weakling King...'

Now the bard recounted the famous argument between Maeve and Aillil about whose possessions were the greater. Finally, the only way to settle it was for them to gather everything they each owned on a great plain for comparison. When the count was made, it was found that a bull of Maeve's had gone over to Aillil's herd because —

> 'He thought it unbecoming in a bull to be
>   managed by a woman!'

This line never failed to produce a roar of laughter. Graunya was too young to appreciate the satire, but she laughed with everyone else. In the same moment, she caught her father's eye and he was looking at her in a curiously speculative manner which made her feel uneasy, as though she had done wrong to laugh. She saw him place his hand over Cormac's on the table, as though to say,

'This is my son and heir, who will manage all our common possessions without argument. *His* bulls will not stray – because he is a man in the making.'

And, for the first time in her life, Graunya was aware of womanhood as a thing separating her from certain desirable pastures, like a prickly hedge ... She brooded on it, unaware of the song slipping away through heroic feats of arms, crashing in battle, sobbing to final defeat.

> 'Then the Brown Bull of Cooley lay over
>   against the Hill,'

sang O Dugan,

> 'And his great heart broke there.
> Thus, when all this war and Thain had
>   ended,
> In his own lad, 'midst his own hills, he died.'

There was a mighty roar of approval from the crowd but Graunya frowned at her finger-nails. She was faintly dissatisfied with the epic this time. It was not that it had moved her any the less – her throat was still tight with tears – but that, suddenly, she was aware of a great inconsistency in it. *Why* did the noble bull have to die? He had chosen his own kind of freedom. Life seemed a high price to pay for it.

O Dugan leaned over her, his white robe brushing her shoulder.

'Have I displeased you, Graunya?' he asked. 'You did not applaud me.'

Her words came at him with a rush, spilling her thoughts: why, why, *why*? He drew her away from the noisy table where everyone else had already forgotten the story.

'Because,' he said, 'the Cattle Drive happened – not once, but many times. And it will happen again. When we recount facts, Graunya, we cannot expect logic; only fairy-tales have tidy endings. Can you understand me?'

'Yes,' she said slowly. Then, '*When* will it happen again.'

'On a small scale, when your brother, Cormac, comes of age. He will steal a neighbour's cattle to bring on a fight.'

'And is there something bigger than that?'

He pressed his lips together and smiled tightly.

'There is,' he replied, 'when one whole country invades

another and drives its cattle off and shouts, "I am the new chief!" '

'Like the King of England does to Ireland?'

'Like so, exactly,' said the bard. 'Remember, last spring-time, how Henry Tudor wiped out the Geraldines by treachery and took their lands, titles and herds?'

She remembered Silken Thomas and his five uncles. The entire country remembered in its shocked conscious-ness: six members of a semi-royal house gone to the block, the great Kildare estates broken. Now it was the duty of the bards to see that no one ever forgot: it was their voca-tion to keep the flame of resentment burning, just as it was the chanting of O Keenan that had fanned the spark of rebellion in Silken Thomas's soul...

Instinct told the O Malley poet that Graunya was more responsive than either of her brothers, and that her influ-ence, in the end, would be wider than theirs: she would marry the leader of another tribe; she would rear his chil-dren; and she would dominate everyone with whom she came into contact. Even now, with the absurd woollen cap on her cropped head, the vitality of her presence was disturbing.

O Dugan smiled again, thinking of the nickname which her brothers had given her and which the whole island was repeating with a grin. When he shut his mind to the meaning of the tacked-on word, the name had a curi-ously melodic quality for him.

Graunuaile.

～

Her mother aroused her before dawn and helped her to dress in linen chemise, worsted petticoat and long leather jacket slit at the sides – fussing over whether she would be warm enough on the high seas, losing no opportunity to kiss and fondle her. Graunya bore all this with rigid patience, her ears pricking up to every sound of preparation from the harbour.

It was a cool, damp morning. The storm wind had dropped to a steady north-westerly, rare enough here and providential for a voyage to Spain.

'I believe you're not going to miss me at all,' the Lady Margaret said plaintively, fastening her daughter's frieze cloak with a heavy gold brooch under her chin.

The last thing Graunya wanted was a tearful scene with her mother; she, herself, was acutely aware of the pain of parting – it had been with her all night and the previous day – but not by a single sob would she admit to feeling it, in case the adventure were snatched from her.

'I will think of you often, my mother,' she replied, 'and Cormac and I will kneel and pray for you every morning and night. Good-bye. God stay with you!'

She ran out into the morning air and down to the dark strand. Clouds were sifting the first grey light of dawn. Ships and shadows and reflections were a misty jumble in the harbour. The water had a heavy smoothness like oil, and sea-birds flew low or stood motionless on distant rocks.

Men were wading out to the long galleys, carrying oars and bundles of their personal belongings, while curraghs served the bigger ships anchored farther offshore. Women were kissing husbands and sweethearts. Yet, in spite of all the activity, there was a kind of muted quiet. Even the convent bell, when it rang, had an unusual softness.

The chaplain came out and blessed the fleet.

'Come, Graunya,' her father said then, 'Cormac is aboard this half-hour.' He lifted her into a curragh, saying to the oarsman, 'Take her out to the flagship.'

The light craft moved quickly over the water. She

looked back once, saw her father and mother embracing at the sea's edge, the woman's head haloed with the first flush of light from the east. A feeling of panic hammered in her throat: she had to go back — But her father's words came to her, 'Some people ... will have what they want ... whatever the price. *You are one of them.*'

She paid with a gulp and a snuffle.

Cormac was up on the poop-deck of the flagship, shouting and waving.

'Graunya! Hey, Graunya *mhaol!*'

She turned and shook her clenched fist at him as the curragh hove to. Then her attention was captured by the Blue Ensign at the masthead. It was streaming so straight that the emblem of the White Seahorse was undistorted by folds: no legless creature of the deep this, but a rearing animal, maned, deep-chested and hooved, such as the old gods rode across the Atlantic.

And she could almost read the O Malley motto underneath:

Terra Marique Potens – Powerful by Land and Sea.